# The Is  Serenity

## Part 1

# Rise
# &
# Fall

**By**

**Gary Edward Gedall**
**01 08 2015**

**Copyright © Gary Edward Gedall 2015**

Published by

# From Words to Worlds,

## Lausanne, Switzerland

## www.fromwordstoworlds.com

Images synthesized by Boris:
encrypto@hotmail.com

**Print Edition**
**ISBN: 2-940535-22-4**
**ISBN 13: 978-2-940535-22-4**

# By the same Author

## Adventures with the Master

## REMEMBER

**Tasty Bites** (Series – published or in preproduction)
*Face to Face*
*Free 2 Luv*
*Heresy*
*Love you to death*
*Master of all Masters*
*Pandora's Box*
*Shame of a family*
*The Noble Princess*
*The Ugly Barren Fruit Tree*
*The Woman of my Dreams*

## The Island of Serenity, Pt 1 Destruction

(Series – published or in preproduction)

Non Fiction -     (published or in preproduction)

The Zen approach to Low Impact Training and Sports

The Zen approach to Modern Living
    Vol 1 Fundamentals, Family & Friends
    Vol 2. Work, Rest & Play
    Vol 3 Life Cycle

**Picturing the Mind:**
    Vol 1          **Basic Principals**
    Vol 2          **Fields within Fields**
    Vol 3          **Pathology, classical, traditional
                   and alternative healing methods**

## Disclaimer:

The characters and events related in my books are a synthesis of all
that I have seen and done, the people that I have met and their
stories. Hence, there are events and people that have echoes with real
people and real events, however no character is taken purely from
any one person and is in no way intended to depict any person, living
or dead.

My books are not, in any way a therapy books and are not meant to
contradict or invalidate, any other vision of the human being or their
psyche, nor any particular therapy.

Contents:

## 1. Taste of the Big Apple

My first lodging was at Sloane House the W34th Street, YMCA, a huge 14 story monstrosity of a building, on the corner of $34^{th}$ and $9^{th}$. I stayed there for several weeks while I was sorting stuff out.

Stuff being, first and foremost my finances. J.J. had not wanted to give me all the money for my trip in cash.

In fact, he chose to give me very little, fearing that I would get ripped off, even travellers checks were not safe enough.

What he had decided was that when I would get to Manhattan, I was to set myself up a bank account, then he could wire me money across on a weekly basis, so that I couldn't just take all the money out in the first week, spend it and then have to ask him for more.

Of course, setting up a bank account as a foreigner in the US, without a social security number, is totally impossible.

After, several frantic transatlantic phone calls, J.J. managed to find a branch of Citibank in London that accepted for him to open an account in both our names and for me to get a check book, which was handed over personally to me by the Assistant Vice President of Citibank in New York.

By the way, the Citibank Plaza in New York is totally wonderful.

Outside, it is a glass and concrete block, not that different than many other, similar buildings.

However, when you enter, you find that it is hollow inside with a huge sunken terrace.

All around this secret plaza, there are restaurants and snack bars and then there is a vast open space in the middle, where you would take your meal or drink to consume.

It has trees and seems almost like you were eating outside in the park.

I remember this coffee shop that sold a drink call Ambrosia, (I think), coffee, whipped cream, chocolate bits, really the food of the Gods, (even if it actually it is a drink).

It was during these first few weeks in New York that I had my first real encounter with NYC.

I had been to a bar and was working on picking up this local girl, a curvy brunette.

She lived somewhere on the upper west side, and I thought that I was going to get off with her that very night.

We talked and we drank, although I was not as generous as I might have been, seeing that I had a very limited amount of cash left, since the money was still not arriving.

We left the bar some time before midnight, and I offered to walk her home, fully expecting not to have to walk back until the morning.

We arrived at her hotel cum apartment house, I was very impressed to see that there was a doorman, receptionist waiting to let us in.

Only, it wasn't us, it was just her, she turned towards me, gave me a quick peck on the cheek, thanked me for the drinks, and disappeared into the old building.

I hesitated for a moment or two, realizing that I would have to succeed to pass by this guy, who didn't look like he wanted to be 'passed by', before even getting a chance to try and sweet talk the girl.

A girl who didn't look to have wanted to have been 'sweet-talked to' either.

So I gave it up and skulked back to my little room at the 'Y', only not.

The 'Y' was already closed for the night.

Not being a hotel, it didn't work on the usual system, if you had not already organized to come in after hours, it was impossible.

Of course I tried, but it was to no avail, no admittance until 08:00 the next morning.

And so, there I was, 18 years old, a few days in the States and stuck on New York's city streets after midnight.

No credit card, very little cash, (I had already paid for two weeks stay in the 'Y' in advance).

With so little means, booking myself into one of the inviting hotels on 34th street was just not an option.

I certainly wasn't feeling groovy and the whores on 34th street, although really nice and friendly, didn't have any useful suggestions for me, other than to stay away from Upper Broadway, after 1 a.m.

I carried on walking down to 7th and then right and carried on to 31st and turned right again.

Almost immediately I found myself standing next to Penn station, and there were lights everywhere. It was my Shangri-La, a haven of light in the dark gloominess of early morning New York.

The first thing that I had to do was to hunt out the toilets, which was slightly scary, seeing the flotsam and jetsam that the city had dumped down those stairs.

Maybe it was intentional; some sort of unspoken agreement to keep the streets fairly clear of this human debris.

Being mid-summer, the night was fairly warm, so I sat on the small wall near the stairs, with my right hand, crammed into my trousers' pocket where my almost empty wallet, was being protected with all my attention.

Although they were particularly rough, unwashed and unshaved, (that went for the women too!), they were in no way aggressive or threatening.

In truth, I must have dozed off, several times, for who knows how long, and nothing untoward happened at all.

At some moment the sun must have risen, for I found myself being pushed aside by the early morning commuters.

I got to my feet, schlepped, (good NYC term), myself over to the 'Y', now fully open and welcoming.

I stuffed myself with a 'healthy', (meaning copious and greasy), breakfast, and found my way to the peace and safety of my postage size, now totally wonderful, room and bed.

By the time the money started coming through I had found a grotty hotel – apartment house, on 74th between Columbus and Amsterdam.

The concept of hotel – apartment is something that I had never heard of before coming to the 'states',

I don't know if it exists in other American cities, but it seems quite normal in the Big Apple.

Take a reasonably nice hotel, of small or medium size, age it 50 to 100 years without any effort to keep it refurbished; neither the entrance, nor the stairways, nor the passages, nor the rooms and especially not the bath rooms, (most would succeed to get an historical protection order in the UK).

Now take a normal sized, (rather dingy), hotel room add the cheapest, ugliest kitchen corner that can be found in the developed world and there you go, a typical hotel-apartment, New York style.

I went to small general store and bought (surprisingly inexpensively), a 'dish-set', cutlery, and pans. Then some cereal, milk, eggs, bread, butter, peanut butter, jam, (jelly), tea and coffee, and set up home.

The milk, butter and stuff looked totally lost and miserable in the oversized 'apartment' fridge, which pretty much dominated the room.

One thing that I had forgotten to buy was a decent (bread) cutting knife, which led to one of my more amusing exchanges with a New York baker.

It was the first Sunday morning and I had run out of bread, but I wasn't worried as I had heard that the bakeries were open on Sunday mornings.

I was looking forward to a crusty Jewish bagel, which I hadn't tasted since J.J. took us on a week's holiday to London, many, many moons ago.

So I go out my hotel, the concierge has directed me to a bakery on Amsterdam, not ten minutes away.

So I 'schlep', (sorry, but I love that word), my way in the early morning sunshine, three long blocks until I see the sign of the Promised Land, 'Benjamin's Bargain Bagel Emporium'.

Whether it was large or small, was hard to make out, it was so full of people.

I elbowed my way to the counter, "could I have some bagels, please."

"Sure, which ones do you want?" It was only then, having arrived at the counter that I remarked that there must have been ten different types of bagels.

Normal, onion, sesame, poppy, salt, white, mi-brown, brown, as well as others that I can't now remember.

So I bought myself five different bagels to try and was just about to leave the shop, when I remembered my lack of an appropriate bread knife. So I made my way back to the counter again, after some minutes, the man returned to me.

"Yes?"

"Sorry, but I don't have a bread knife at home, could I trouble you to cut the bagels for me?"

"Here, take this, and have a nice day," he thrust an object into my hand, I looked down at it, not knowing if he was making fun of me, or what. In my hand I was holding, a thin, white, plastic, throw away knife.

"But I need to cut my bagels," I was back again at the counter.

"Here," he gestured towards my bag, which I handed to him. He chose a bagel at random and pulled it out of the bag, and then, with the thin, plastic knife, he proceeded to cut open my bagel.

Of course London bagels have very hard crusts, but New York style bagels can be opened with a thin, white plastic, throw away knife, so now you know.

My apartment was only a few minutes' walk from Central Park and it was the period of the 'new' roller skates, which had big, white wheels, ball Barings, and were the things to have.

So I bought myself a pair and taught myself how to skate, in the sacred heart of New York.

Being young, free and English, skating, (and falling quite a lot), around Central Park, it was not difficult to fall into conversation with many a pretty young American, and I certainly didn't miss many opportunities.

Angelique had sold me out to the enemy, which is to say, my parents, so flirting and sleeping with these girls, was only my way to get back some self-esteem, and to take some distance.

I roller skated a lot, made out as often as I could, ate out from time to time, and caught a few Broadway and off Broadway shows.

Once I got a pair of 'twofies' (two for one tickets), to go and see 'Oh Calcutta', so I took a girl. The show wasn't that hot, everyone took their clothes off right at the beginning.

After that there wasn't that much interest, although we almost made out in the theatre, but for some busybody usher that flashed a torch on us at just the wrong moment.

We didn't get to see the second act, but we sure made up for it when we got back to my grotty, love nest.

After all, it wasn't so bad, one quite quickly got used to the grottiness, the bath room really took some getting used to.

That and having to always remember to check your shoes before putting them on, that, or not minding sharing your shoe with a cockroach!

My stay in New York passed all too quickly, but now I was re-resourced and ready to face the next chapter of my life.

Aston Business School, one of the top business schools in Europe, in the centre of England, in the heart in Birmingham.

## 2.    The Visitor

"Can I help you?" She looks up from the patient chart that she was in the process of updating.

"I am coming to see one of your patients," he fumbles in his maroon robes and pulls out a folded piece of paper.

His accent is difficult to place; and his English is not quite perfect. There were quite a lot of young doctors from India, who had similar accents, and turns of phrase, but he didn't sound exactly like them either.

"I'm sorry, but visiting hours are over for today. They shouldn't have let you up. I will have to call reception and have someone escort you out."

"But …"

"And more than that, this is a private wing, I could get into serious trouble just you being here.

And you being here, in the nurse's office, well that is against all the hospital rules.

These are medical secrets, you know?" She waves vaguely over the mess of papers and charts that litter the small, Formica topped desk."

"Oh, I am so very sorry, I do most apologise. I never meant to be doing any harm, I just wanted to ask you where to find Mr. Ferguson."

"Hello? Who's that? … Hi, Jane Cooper ward 14. Listen, did you let some weird guy in brown robes in, to visit someone?

… A what? … A letter of authority? I've never heard of nothing like that. … Okay, alright, I'm not saying that you done som'art wrong, just that maybe, wouldn't have been such a bad idea to ask. …

To ask someone before sending some weirdo up to a private ward at eleven o'clock at night, don't y' think?"

She takes the phone from her ear and looks at it, as if the phone was the person that she was talking to.

The look says something like, 'why don't they make the effort to employ people that have higher IQ's than zoo monkeys?'

"She says that you have some sort of letter," he again takes it to give to her, "but even if it's signed by the bloody Queen, I still wouldn't have the authority to let you into any of the patient's rooms."

So saying so, she carefully smooths her white, nurse's uniform. Something in the familiar gesture, always helps her to relax and calm down.

This uniform, is, for her, proof of her ability to break out of the squalid world of her grubby, council estate childhood.

The uniform is always perfectly cleaned and ironed, just as her hair is always washed and tied back in a tight ponytail, with the sides carefully pinned into place.

Never a single, solitary strand could accidently stray across her surgically, scrubbed, lightly freckled face.

"But what am to do? Please, I have to be seeing him tonight."

"Why tonight? Why can't you just come back tomorro' when the day staff are here and you can ask the duty doctor for permission?"

"I am sorry to trouble you so much, but have to be taking an aeroplane tomorrow morning, and if I am to come back, and for quite a long time, there are many things that I will have to be arranging."

"If you come back?" Without understanding anything that he is referring to, she is, just the same intrigued.

"If I agree to undertake the treatment."

"Treatment?" She goes over to her desk, pulls open a draw of hanging files and hunts out the one of the person in question.

"Sorry mate, but there's no treatment planned for this one, there's nawt to do for the poor bugger. You'd be just wasting your time."

"But I have a letter."

She looks at him and then back at the phone, tonight all the brain surgeons have gone home to bed, and all she has left to deal with, are their failures.

"Look, I'm not supposed to tell you this, medical secret and all, but what the Hell?

Your Mr. Ferguson is in a coma, has been for a while, and is not likely to wake up, like not never."

"Please Miss, I have a letter."

"You're a stubborn one, aren't you?"

Quite unexpectedly, his lips part in a shy smile.

"I have heard others saying the same thing."

Did that sketch of a smile remind her of her nan, or of someone else, or nobody in particular?

In any case, she felt herself warming to the strange older man. Older man, as it was very difficult with his woollen cap covering his hair and thick beard to clearly guess his real age.

"I'll have to call the duty doctor."

"So there is also a duty doctor at night?"

"Why of course ... I'll just call him, please could you just wait outside?"

"I'm not supposed to be being inside of your office, I'm very sorry to have intruded." He leaves, gently closing the door behind him.

She picks up the phone and dials a number and immediately replaces the handset. She turns to the man and waves him over towards some chairs that are placed against the lemon coloured wall.

Without waiting to see the outcome of her gesture, she pushes some papers away from the corner of the desk and sits herself down on it. One by one, her nails are inspected for shape and cleanliness.

There is no need, she has already filed and scrubbed them earlier this evening before starting her shift, but it is also an unconscious habit.

Waiting for the doctor to respond to his beep, there is no sense in doing anything other than wait, and waiting often means checking one's nails.

If she would have time to think things through, she would have rushed quickly to the toilets to check on her makeup; discrete, but carefully applied. The duty doctor was a young, handsome Scot.

He had joked that they might be related, as they had the same freckles. He had smiled a reckless, rakish, roguish smile. Of course she was in love with him.

The phone makes her jump, but she only takes a moment to respond. She grabs the handset and brings it her mouth, her mouth smiles and slightly breathless,

"Hello."

If the gesture might have reminded one of someone bringing a fresh, cream doughnut towards their famished body, then, unfortunately, in this case, the cream must have been, dreadfully off.

The smile is immediately replaced by a rather sour look. She talks for a few moments, nods, once or twice, and then, a little sulkily, replaces the phone.

As she comes to open the office door, he, who has been quietly watching the whole scene, gets up and comes to her.

"The doctor will be coming shortly."

"Is there something wrong?"

"Wrong? Why would there be something wrong?"

"You seemed to be upset by something."

"What you talking about?" Her use of correct English, clearly falters.

"Oh, I'm sorry, I have intruded again. Please to accept my apologies."

"I don't know what you're talking about."

"Then I must be, of course, mistaken. No harm done?"

"No, no harm done. Could you please go and sit down, I have to carry on updating the charts. The doctor will be with you shortly."

"Yes, thank you, you have already informed me. I will now go and sit down and wait patiently, and not disturb you further." He makes a type of little bow and returns to his seat."

## 3. Aston, 1st Year

I had organized to arrive back to the house a week before Uni started, (actually Fresher's Week, if one wishes to be anal about it).

There was a pile of stuff that was waiting for me; a mass of books to buy, some forms to fill in, my room allocation, 13, 13 Lawrence Tower, (don't bother to go looking for it, they blew it up, some years ago), and, oh yes, the results of my highers.

Maths, B, Economics C and Further Maths E, I would have been screwed if it wasn't for General Studies, which thanks my perfect results in French gave me another B.

All in all, I had comfortably succeeded the average needed to enter Aston.

(Of course I could have taken French and aced it, but my parents put a block on that, arguing that my level was already so high, it would have been two years wasted, so I had to slog it with the maths).

J.J. took me up to London for a couple of days, and we did the Dragon Alley bit and bought the necessary for my new academic life.

Arriving in Birmingham was a bit of a culture shock, to me it seemed very exciting but at the same time particularly grotty. However, there were some wonderful compensations.

Not only had Mike made the obvious decision to follow me to Aston, but Duncan, had chosen, knowing our plans, to take a year 'off', (working quite hard so it seems), so as to start at the same time as us, so the three Musketeers, were once again reconstituted.

Lawrence tower was already pretty old and miserable by that time, it was an oldish tower of about twenty floors, with each floor having three wings, like the inside spokes of a wheel.

Thirteen, thirteen, was, no surprises here, room number thirteen on floor thirteen, unlucky for some.

This was possibly quite true as it was the room next door to the communal kitchen and facing the bathrooms, it certainly wasn't the quietest room on the floor.

The floors were meant to be single sex, but that didn't deter some of the final year students, (the towers were reserved for first years and final year students), to share their enormous room's, (about six feet by nine feet – even monks get more than that!), with their girl-friends.

In general, this didn't cause any real problems.

Only, from time to time the shower was unavailable due to a female presence. –

I do admit there was one girlfriend that I used to fantasize, accidently walking in on …

The first year was okay, I chose Aston because it's Management and Admin Sciences Course covers all the different aspects of Business.

Subjects that were covered in the first year included; Sociology, Psychology, Law, (Penal and Contract), Statistical Methods and Economics.

Nothing was too deeply entered into and there was plenty of time to get pissed and try picking up the Uni girls.

As the first year was common to all the MAS students we were all together for the whole year, which unfortunately, didn't continue into the later years.

Mike then chose to specialize in Accounting and Economics.

Duncan, lent more towards personnel management, business psychology, HR stuff.

I was more into Marketing, (my major), although I did follow a lot of Duncan's psychology courses, (they were a bit of a soft option).

I also took a module of planning, stocking, delivery and such, which was so stupid and obvious that I slept through most of it, but that was in the final year, I'm getting a little ahead of myself.

Being fairly intelligent, but not very hard working, I quickly found myself in the middle grades for the year.

These, very average results were to be my norm for most of my university career.

It seemed to worry Duncan, much more than me.

He pushed himself to finish the first year with the equivalent of a first.

My time in students union, when I might well have been studying, meant that I was happy enough to finish the first year in the 2:2 grade band.

# 4. 2nd & 3rd Years

As, for the second year we were obliged to find accommodation off campus.

I left the boring details of house hunting to Mike.

He phoned me to ask for me to wire him the deposit to him, as he had found a jewel of a house, inexpensive but a little ways away from the centre of Birmingham.

The house was a tiny semi-detached, unloved and uncared for, in a lost world named Crabbs Cross, Redditch,

This quaint village of several dozen miserable blocks of terraced houses was conveniently located only 15 miles away from the Aston campus by bus.

Being a good hour away from Uni, it was not surprising that we didn't return every evening.

In fact, to meet up with Mike, in the house was a pretty rare occurrence indeed.

During the first week of the new term, I fell in with a really weird guy who called himself Abdul.

The was more than likely borrowed from someone or somewhere, as he was white and English.

He had created an insomniac society, using the university chaplain's building, (heaven knows how he managed to swing that little miracle).

He kept it officially open and functioning between 11:00 pm and 04:00 am, but on many occasions we just crashed out there until the morning.

As for Duncan, he was almost always shacked up with some girl or other, and we only saw him when we had joint courses together.

The second year was okay, I also discovered the Aston Arts Centre, and started appearing in quite a lot of plays.

Other than these, more interesting facts, the rest of the academic year passed without much incident or (none theatrical), drama.

You might well notice that I've not mentioned much of my time during the holidays.

Well there's not that much to say. I would go back to the house, take a pile of books to read, and keep as far away from everyone as possible.

I would avoid going into the village, as I had no wish to cross Angelique or the baby or her parents.

My parents tried to be civil, J.J. would often invite me to the pub for drinks, but I just shook my head and returned to my reading.

Maman would monologue with me, keeping up a one-sided conversation during the moments when we had to be together, meals and such.

Jean Jacques had long since cut all relationship cords with me, we would look through each other as if we were already two ex-corporeal, ghostly beings.

For the summer holidays I found myself a place in a stables not far from the village.

It was J.J. that relayed Mike's message to me, and sorted out the money for the house deposit.

When the second summer arrived, I was already organized for my industrial placement year, I had decided to find my own placement and placed an ad in the Times.

By some odd set of circumstances, the guy that responded had bought some parts for his factory from J.J.

So they knew each other, from there on, getting the job, was just a formality.

The job only lasted five months, the factory owner was a total lunatic.

After a slight misunderstanding, (I told a client the truth that is order had not as yet be started), he sacked me on the spot.

As it was a Friday morning, I found myself, six hours later, with three weeks' pay in hand and no more internship.

Fortunately, just before I was thrown out of Uni for not completing my training year, I secured a Trainee Manager position at Hamley's Toy Shop, and all finished well.

I spent the summer on a student exchange, back in the US, working in a pleasure beach in Asbury Park, New Jersey. I re-contacted one of my New York girl-friends and the summer passed very well indeed.

## 5. Final Year & Graduation

For our final year, we managed to organize a mini-flat on campus for the three of us, which we obviously christened the 'Three Musketeers' Coffee Shop'.

As we were all majoring in different specialties, (mine was Marketing, Duncan in Industrial Psychology and Human Resources and Mike in Economics and Accountancy), there were few courses that we took together.

Being also interested in psychology, Duncan and I had some joint courses, but the only course that we all took was the compulsory business and marketing computer simulation.

The university was quite advanced with computing at that time, it had a large and thriving computer department.

Hence it was financially well enough endowed to afford an expensive computer business simulation package.

Each student joined into one of fifteen teams of about ten. Each team was given a 'company' to direct, on all levels; production, finance, marketing, distribution, etc.

We started the simulation with; one small factory, a lump of cash and our own, local market in which we sold the products that we produced.

From there on, each week, we had to decide on our business strategy for the next 'quarter'.

Which was to say; how much to invest into production, marketing, infrastructure, (administration, transport and the like).

Also, whether to expand or re-enforce our markets.

Whether to invest money into our existing regions or new territories, or just to sit tight, and accumulate cash reserves.

Or to pay off loans, and wait for an interesting opportunity in the next quarter.

Of course, the interest lay in the fact that we were not alone in the market for our products, we had any of fourteen other companies, vying for the same clients, possibly several, in the same territory.

As with any game of strategy where there are several protagonists, there also exists the possibilities for alliances and joint actions.

I had a good friend, Bonny, (quite a juicy blonde, to explain a bit our friendship), who was on one of the other teams and opened up the possibility for some discrete sharing of information.

Our team met up on Friday mornings, giving someone the time to fill in the action report, before the seven o'clock deadline.

That was when the sheets were collected so the data could be entered during the week-end, (some lucky students found this a quite well paid Saturday job).

The results could then be processed during the rest of the week-end, printed and posted out for Monday lunch time.

(As you might notice, things took rather a lot more time, in those days.)

The teams would then have the whole week to meet and plan the strategy for the next quarter.

One of Bonny's group had informed us that they were going to invest heavily into a new region relatively close to one of their existing factories.

They would then release to us a sector that, even though they had a good market share, was proving too expensive on the level of distribution.

(The reason that they had invested so much into this region was that they had found a huge marketing opportunity when one of the other teams had 'gone under').

Our group, which had a factory much closer, were very keen to exploit that opportunity.

So we had voted to heavily increase production in that factory and to invest in a massive advertising campaign, for that territory.

The form was filled out then and there, and as almost of the group were leaving campus early, to leave for the week-end, I was left with the task of dropping in the form during the afternoon.

I had finished my last lecture and had just popped into the Students Union for a quick half before strolling over to the office to post the report, when I bumped into Bonny.

(Not literally, but I'm sure that she wouldn't hold it against me).

"Just off to post our rapport," I opened the conversation with something neutral.

"It's a good thing that Rob, told you of the changes, isn't it?" She responded lightly.

"What changes? Rob's not told me of any changes," a certain note of concern colouring my voice.

"Oh shit, he didn't tell then?" Now she was expressing a certain level of tension.

"Tell me what?"

"About the changes."

"What Bloody changes?"

"Don't shout at me, is wasn't me that was supposed to tell you."

"Sorry, cool down."

"You don't get to shout at me, it's not my fault."

"Okay, I'm sorry, I'm really sorry. I shouldn't have shouted. Now, here take a drink of my beer. Good, now, okay, what changes?"

"It's the simulation. Our group was going to give up sector 4, and focus on sector 16."

"Which is sector 4 and sector 16?"

"Which are sectors 4 and 16?"

"Fuck the grammar Bonny, what are you trying to say?"

"Will's team are going to build a mega factory between our main factory and the sector that we were going to give up.

If we move out of that sector now, in the next quarter they will monopolise that sector, and eventually eat up all the sectors in between.

Then they will undercut our prices through economies of scale and low transport costs."

"So what have you decided to do?"

"We're investing in building a big factory in the sector, and will continue our advertising and sales, even slightly cutting the selling price.

Even if we make a loss in this quarter, by next quarter we'll have a producing factory and a full order book.

Will's team might have their mega-factory, but we will already have all the market, they'll be totally in the shit."

"Sure," my brain had started to function again, "and so will we. We've committed to an important advertising campaign to take over your clients, and have upped the production in our factory in sector, sector, the one next door to there."

"That's why Rob was supposed to tell Mike, so you could change strategies."

"It's a bit fucking late now, we're screwed."

"Well, I'm sorry, but it's really not my fault."

"No, it's not your fault, I've got to go."

I honestly didn't know what to do, it seemed pointless to post the form, as it was.

It would put is in an impossible position in which there was no way to compete and win.

So I went back to our little flat, (number 4, Bishop Ryder House, if memory serves me well), and wondered what to do.

Suddenly it came to me, I thrust open the window, and shouted out into the cooling air.

'Group 10, this is Jamie Ferguson, and I'm calling an emergency meeting of our group, the meeting will begin in five minutes'.

I then closed the window, put the kettle on to make myself a cup of tea, and went and fetched a new, virgin form.

'So,' I discussed with the group members present, (which just happened to be only me), 'we need to take into account the new that we have.

If Will's group are going to invest in a mega factory they're not going to be thinking about doing much advertising in their home turf.

(It was rare that another group would try and encroach on another groups' base territory, after all they had a factory there, and had their local clients since the first quarter).

'So why don't we launch a killer assault, big advertising bucks, just undercutting their usual selling price, prioritising our stock distribution to that sector and see what that does to their cash flow?'

I waited to see if there would be any dissenting voices, not so surprisingly, there were none.

So I agreed and instructed the scribe in true Star trek fashion, to, 'make it so.'

I arrived only minutes before the student, assigned to collect the forms, emptied the box.

Monday brought with it cold, drizzly rain, (what do you expect, this Birmingham, after all), and a huge torrent of abuse.

Many of the group were just upset that I had acted totally alone, they just refused to hear that I had no choice but to act alone.

It wasn't my fault that I had only just heard about the change of plans an hour or so before the forms had to handed in.

Don't forget, this was long, long before portable phones and the like, I really had no way to contact them.

But that was not the worst of it, you see, my little strategy of attacking the home sector of Will's group, had important consequences.

With a massive advertising campaign, low prices and all the available stock from our three factories, meant that they sold virtually nothing in their main market.

Then there was the decision of Bonny's team to stay in the other market and build a factory, where Will's team had just taken the decision to borrow a particularly large amount of money for their mega factory.

That and the advertising campaign with low selling price that Bonny's team had put into place, meant that Will's group sold almost nothing that quarter.

Their cash flow had fallen below critical, and they had been forced into bankruptcy!

Duncan was livid, "that's not how we function. We are here to win fairly, not to humiliate and destroy the opposition.

It's just a game, you don't have to do things like that. This is also my group, how am I supposed to look the others in the face, after dealing such an underhand trick?"

"But it is just a game, and we are supposed to do our best to win. This could take my average from a 2:2 to a 2:1, and you, you could well end up with a first."

"If I end up with a first it will be through hard work, not attacking others unfairly."

Fortunately there was at least one member of the group on my side, little Mike was dancing so much, I was worried that he would pee himself.

"That was brilliant. Brilliant, brilliant, brilliant. I've always known that you could do things like that."

"What do you mean?"

"Oh, don't let's talk on that now, let me offer you a drink. And there wasn't even a dollar bet that you couldn't do it."

I must admit that the reference was lost to me, but I gladly accepted the drink and the praise.

Some of the other students gave me a bit of the cold shoulder, but I did get a few free drinks in the Sack o' Potatoes, later that night.

My intervention took my group up into the top three, but it seems that some members of the other teams had been coached by friends that had graduated the year before and they knew of some glitches in the system that finally turned the odds in their favour.

But what was most troubling was that noble and honest side of Duncan, if we were to go into business, the three of us, would that Christian upbringing prove to be our downfall?

Unfortunately, it would.

Final exams were soon looming up like some ugly unpaid debt that we were supposed to have already started saving up for, many months before.

It was the Easter holidays; a few of the final year students had gone home to study, many had stayed on campus, to be near the library and the few comrades that had diligently taken notes throughout the year.

I had decided to screw all that and had inscribed to play in the musical show, 'Cabaret'.

The rehearsals were to be during these holidays and it was set to go up early in the last term.

The fact that I was in a play, only a few weeks before my finals, succeeded to freak out some of my profs.

Actually it freaked them out enough for them to come down to the Arts Centre and threaten me that if I failed my finals, I could not blame the play.

As the degree grades were an average of the second year exams, continual assessment over the final year and the final exams, doing the maths, I would need to fail just about every exam to descend my average from a 2:2 to a 3$^{rd}$. So I didn't sweat it.

Not that I can sing nor dance, but acting in Cabaret was fun, and I enjoyed riling up the profs.

So the finals came and went, I got my 2:2 as expected, Duncan got his 2:1 and Mike settled also for a 2:2.

Maman and J.J. came up for the ceremony, I almost cracked and allowed Jean Jacques to come, but in the end, I decided that he didn't deserve to share my graduation.

For the shortest of moments, I had the feeling that my parents were proud of me.

They gladly posed for multiple photographs with me in my cap and gown, and it seemed that all was well.

Until…

"Right lad, now you've got your piece o' paper, it'll be time for you to start to do some real work."

So, that was it, the first of our family to succeed to earn an Honours Degree from an English University, and all that I get is that? 'Your piece o' paper'.

As for Maman, it was only when I happened to notice my photograph in our local rag.

It was then that I realised why she was so open to taking so many photographs of us, she wanted to be totally sure that she would finish with one that did her justice.

I was also naïve enough to not have noticed that she positioned herself in between me and the camera.

Which meant that I, the supposed hero of the story, was half masked by the 'proudest mother in the world'.

Not that that meant that much to me, it was just more irritation to add to my sack of irritations that was my experience of family.

## 6. The Visit

The click, click of someone walking towards him, signals the likelihood of the doctor, being on her way.

Being rather small, yet also being particularly aware of her importance, wearing some form of heel is obligatory.

Not that shifts of, often over twelve hours, aren't rather hard on one's feet, but she had been wearing heels since she was fourteen, for her, it is totally normal.

Nurse Jane Cooper, also hears her approaching. Nurse Jane Cooper is doing her best to hide her disappointment that the duty doctor that she expected, was not this Italian bitch, but her smooth, Scottish sex dream.

Nurse Jane Cooper, was even irritated that old, weird geezer, had noticed just how disappointed that she was, as soon as she realised who the duty doctor was.

Doctor Paola Russo pushes open the half glass door of the office.

She must have seen the man sitting patiently on the hard, plastic chair.

Especially, as he started to get up as she came towards him.

It was only when he realised that she was intentionally looking straight through him that he disappeared back into the chair.

The door is closed quietly, but firmly. Doctor Russo might be annoyed at being disturbed during one of her few moments of break.

Yes she might, but she is much too well educated to let an outsider hear her tear strips of this thoughtless nurse.

However, this is a nurse from the estates, tearing strips off of her, even with the authority of a doctor, isn't quite so easy.

The audience to this silent, screening, seen from outside of the office, is enjoying an interesting spectacle.

The nurse, who stood up politely, when the doctor first came in, now seems to start to shrink down as the other begins to talk.

And, to be strictly honest, to gesticulate, in a rather energetic fashion.

The use of modern sign language, has nothing to say to the use of the hands by our Mediterranean neighbours.

Shrink, shrink, shrink, and then, like a white clad, orange speckled, jack-in-the-box, she shoots back up, and towers over her raven haired, superior.

The little doctor, attempts to increase her height, but to little avail.

So, lacking any other course of action, she throws her hands up, as a sign of resignation, turns and exists the office.

"So, what is it exactly that you want?"

"I have a letter," he responds, politely.

"So, let us see this letter."

"You want to see the letter?" He is surprised, that at last, someone is willing to read this document.

"Well, you have been waving it under people's noses all night."

"Please, read," he fishes out the letter and passes it to her.

She takes the thin, black rimmed glasses, hanging by a cord, around her neck, pushes them into her nose and quickly scans the note.

"So you are a monk?"

"Yes, I have been called that."

"Well that, is what they call you here.

So, the family of Mr. Ferguson, think that you can do something to awaken their sleeping princess?"

"It is a man, Mr. Ferguson?"

"Yeh, yeh. So what magic are you thinking to perform in our little hospital?"

"I do not do magic, I am but a simple man. I am here tonight to see Mr. Ferguson, to see if I believe that I might be able to something to help him."

The doctor looks at him rather sceptically.

"I really don't see what you could possibly do to help, nor would the hospital authorities be open to you carrying out any alternative interventions, within the hospital establishment, so I ..."

"You could convince them to switch of the life support."

The doctor turns and gives a withering look to the young nurse.

"Well, there's not much chance of him coming out of it, not after all this time.

And you're right, there's surely nothing much that he could do, it's just not worth, not even to bother to take the time to look."

"Thank you Nurse Cooper, I will be the judge of whether or not to allow this person, to assess Mr. Ferguson. …

Yes, your letter is in order, I will give you the authorisation to examine this patient."

Nurse Cooper turns to return to her paperwork; but, maybe, just maybe, the man fancies that he catches, just the merest flash of a wink, as her head turns, before, it is gone.

## 7.  The Keys to the Kingdom

They, (who 'they' were, I was never to clearly discover), but these all powerful beings, had named her Aideen.

Aideen Miller to give her, her full title.

It seems that Aideen means 'little fire', which admittedly proved more than appropriate for she was a little spitfire, she also had the same flaming red hair of Angelique.

What she had acquired from our side of the family, my mother's to be exact, was the shape of the eyes and her nose, giving that bird like impression.

Only her eyes were not always the deep brown of the Armatage's, when she would get angry they would take on a weird Irish green tint.

If anything it then made her look even more like a bird.

So how, you might ask, can I, threatened with immediate and sever poverty, if I would even approach mother or child, gather such intimate and complete knowledge?

From one of the most unlikely of sources, from the alcoholically disinhibited mouth of J.J. himself.

It only took a couple of double whiskeys to totally liberate his tongue.

It seemed that he was taking more than a passing interest in the health and welfare of his first grandchild.

However, that benevolent, paternal attitude did nothing to soften his resolve to not allow me any access to her or Angelique.

"Y' just ha' t'accept the fact that y' canna' see her," his accent accentuating with the volume of Scottish whiskey imbibed.

"But why not? You came from a working class background."

"I," he looked me hard in the eye, straightened himself up as best he could, not easy in his condition, "am the offspring of royalty."

One of positive facets of J.J. was his pleasure to debate.

He had always accepted and supported our right to disagree with him, as long as we could find a valid argument, to defend our own positions.

This meant that when he would come up with a statement, I was primed to think up a repost.

"And what is there to say that she is not also descended from royalty?

At the same time that your far relative was having hanky-panky with her king.

Then, there were many, many small kingdoms in Ireland, she could very easily be descended from one of those royal houses."

He stopped to think for a moment, too long, he was supposed to come back within thirty seconds, over that time meant that had no answer.

I could smell victory looming up, like a 50 centimetre bass, erupting from an icy lake, as I continue to reel it in.

Come on J.J., it's time to reel you in, so I can take you home and claim my victory.

"Anyway, you're na way mature enough to take the responsibility?"

"Say what?"

"Even wi' y' famous bit o' paper, you've no idea what the world is abou', ya' go an' prove y'se' t' be a man, an' then we'll see."

Okay, so he snatched my victory from out from under my very nose. The famous slip 'twixt the cup and the lip', but he'd not managed to protect himself as fully as before.

The armour now had a chink in it, 'prove yourself to be a man, my son, then the keys to the kingdom of Heaven will be yours.'

"So when I prove myself to be a man, then you will accept for me to take on Angelique and Aideen?"

"When you'll be a man, you wo'na need me for anything, so do what you will, will be the whole o' the law. Come, it's late, one of us has t' go t' work tommora."

And that is how I get the door to my future unlocked, all I had to do now was to find the means to push it open.

## 8. The Monk who bought himself a Mini

"I've bought myself a motorcar." He was incredibly excited, and again forgot that he was not supposed to be entering into her office.

"Oh, it's you?" Several weeks having passed since his first visit, she had almost totally forgotten about him.

And if, by chance, when administering to her comatose patient, the image of the strange robed man, might cross her mind, she had decided that he was a 'bit of a nutter'.

And had promptly redirected her mind to thinking about other, more important things, like when the Scottish doctor would be next on duty.

"Where have you been?"

Not being one, strictly for protocol, and also being particularly inquisitive by nature, she had also seemed to forget that he was not allowed to be in the office.

And more than that, there were patient charts, protected by the medical secret, strewn all over the small, desk.

"As I am thinking that I must have said, I had to go and arrange a long leave of absence, so that I would have the time to be occupying myself with Mr. Ferguson."

"So it's alright then?"

"Yes, and I have now another letter, this time from your hospital administration, agreeing for me to work with Mr. Ferguson."

"How can you work with him, he's all but dead?"

She responded, maybe a little too quickly and a little too directly.

"Oh, sorry, I shouldn't have said that."

"It's alright, young lady, I can understand your reaction. Mr. Ferguson is, as you say, seeming to be being in a deep coma.

However, what I have to say, is that when I came to see him the last time, I ran a few, how would I say it?

I ran some tests. I needed to know if he was still able to react to my presence and to different vibrations."

"You did tests?"

"Yes, yes of course, why do think that I have accepted to undertake this work?

It would not be being correct to waste everyone's time, and the money of my benefactor.

The very same benefactor, that I might add, who has financed me, my own little car, so that I might carry my bowls, to and from the hospital."

"What bowls?" She was really having problems following this little man's discourse.

"And what tests did you do?"

Her medical curiosity, won out over all the other, unanswered questions in her active, blonde head.

"Come, I will show you, if you wish."

And, not really waiting for an answer, he excitedly strolled out of the office and towards the antiseptically, clean room.

The patient was lying on a series of wide slings, just above the height of the open bed, there are no obvious signs that he is in a long term coma.

There is no feeding tube protruding from his nose, as one often sees in films and such.

As, for long term situations, the feeding tube is inserted directly into the stomach.

Nor does he have any need for oxygenation, as he seems to be able to breathe without.

In short; other than the fact that he doesn't move, one could be convinced that he is simply, deeply, asleep.

"Can you please let him down?"

"Sure, it's about time anyway."

She occupies herself with the pulley system, and gently lowers the inert man, back onto the bed.

"Now watch carefully," he takes out a small tuning fork from the secret folds of his robe.

Striking it gently, but firmly, on the metal bars on the side of the bed, he then places it on a point between and just slightly higher than the line of the man's eyes.

The effect, although quite subtle, is, never-the-less, immediate and noticeable.

From being totally limp, a wave of tension, can be seen, flowing down the coma victim's body.

"Shite! How did you do that?"

The question, is, at the same time, totally ridiculous, but yet, still, perfectly understandable.

The gentle eyes turn towards her, not at all put out by the formulation of the question.

"It seems that our Mr. Ferguson is not as dead as he might seem."

"But he doesn't respond to anything; light, sound, heat, anything."

"If I am understanding correctly, Mr. Ferguson tried to take his own life," she nods.

"And, so he is saying in his suicide note, he does not have the will nor the courage to face the life that he has made.

So, if he was ready to kill himself then, why would he be wanting to revive himself now?"

"Don't know."

"Neither would anyone. In short, I believe that Mr. Ferguson is totally capable to return to our world, he just doesn't want to."

"Then there's nothing to do?"

"If I thought that there was nothing to do, would I be here now?"

"S'pose not. But what can you do?"

"You would be liking me to explain?"

"Sure, would you like a cup o' tea, I think that it must be time for my break, anyway."

"But I'm not allowed to be in your office."

"You are now a recognised collaborator of the hospital, you have every right to be invited into my office, you have an official letter."

## 9. Gifts of Promise

We had all split up after graduation; I went home, as did Mike, but Duncan was offered an open ticket to 'anywhere' as an acknowledgement of his success.

Of course I was happy for his chance to travel, but somewhere I was also jealous and angry.

Jealous, not that he got the ticket, what did I care? I was sure that I could get the means to travel anywhere in the world.

J.J. was not mean, just bloody difficult at times, and as long as I kept away from Angelique and Aideen, he was fine with me.

What I was jealous and angry about were his parents.

His parents acknowledged him and his university degree with honours.

Mine, either took my four years as an excuse to mess about, or simply as a way to further their own self-promotion industry.

That is why I was feeling jealous and angry.

However, Duncan's travels proved to be the door to the Aladdin's cave, through which I was to pass and because of which I was to achieve my greatest successes and my worst failures.

Duncan was gone for almost a month, all told. I spent, or to be more honest, wasted my time, hanging around the house, the village pub and my old tree.

I had succeeded to win back my nature sanctuary, or should we say that Jean Jacques had had the good sense, or dare I say the caring, to respect my difficult life situation and had ceased to frequent the place.

More than that, being sensitive to my determined decision to freeze him out on any occasion that we found ourselves in the same space, he had found a number of friends that he was decided to visit during the rest of his holidays.

Just FYI (for your information), he was now in his second or third year of Law at Glasgow Uni., he had the possibility to study Law at Cambridge, but had turned it down!!

Not only was my brother, as intelligent, (at least), as me, but he was always the good student, so he got the most incredibly good results on his highers.

Now I think about it, J.J. offered him a watch, when he graduated. Not only that, but not just any watch, a fucking expensive Swiss watch, a Hublot.

I didn't think much of it at the time, not until many years later when I chanced to find out what that 'trinket' actually cost.

The unfairness's of my life seem to increase with reflection, it's like a tax inspector checking your books; you know that there's shit in there, but his trained eyes find so much more than you've ever imagined could be there.

Of course there was no way that I couldn't cross Angelique, alone or with Aideen, with the town being so small, and my hanging around as I was.

Both being very aware of the deals that we had been forced to accept from my parents, we feigned to have forgotten to having ever known each other.

As our relationship was based on our meeting around Mary Magdalene, not many people were aware of that, and since we had been prohibited from seeing other by my parents, it would have been many years since we really had spent any time in each other's company.

Added to that, the fact that she had had a bastard child, would, in itself, be enough for me to legitimately choose to act if as I had never known her.

What-ever the reason or reasons, no-one ever seemed to remark on our mutual lack of recognition.

I don't know what she must have felt, if anything, seeing me, there in the flesh, the father of her child, a child that we had conceived in a moment of tenderness, of sharing, of support, of love.

I hope that it bloody hurt, 'cus it certainly hurt me.

She had chosen the easy option to sell out our love; any chance of happiness of me and all contact with my own child.

That I had also agreed to Mephistopheles's soul selling contract, seemed to be irrelevant to me, at that time.

It was only her choice, which she took alone, and before I was presented with the fait accompli.

I couldn't see anything other than her betrayal, I could only feel my own pain.

Fortunately, Duncan returned and rescued me from the awful Tantalus, which was the family that I never had.

Duncan returned full of enthusiasm and gifts, he ran up my room.

"Jus' y' wait 'til ya' see this", he called down from the stairs.

Two minutes later he was descending them again, but this time with most of his hairy, Scottish legs on show.

"What do you think of that?" He gestured down to the flimsy scrap of coloured material, somehow wrapped around his toned waist, "it's an Indonesian kilt!"

"It's a skirt, you berk, why are you wearing a skirt, is there something that I should know? You know I'm open to all sorts of shit, you know you can tell me."

"You Jessie, this is a Lungi, or as the Indonesians call it, a Sarung."

"But women wear sarongs."

"This is a man's SarUng", he smiled back, heavily emphasising the pronunciation.

"Fine, why are you wearing it?"

"Because it's comfortable".

"I'd love to see you wearing that walking down Oxford St."

"Is that a dare?" He would as well.

"I hope that you've brought me back something better than that."

"Here", he dove into his bag and carefully brought out a little package, heavily wrapped. It was quite heavy for its size.

"It's not a crucifix, is it?" I could feel the tell-tale form of the cross, even through the packaging.

"No, it's certainly not a crucifix."

"Oh, it's a knife, but what's this with the blade, it's all wavy, what bloody use is this? Is this another of your little jokes?"

"James, hold it carefully, it's a sacred knife, it's called a Kris, and it's an important ceremonial object."

"Serious?"

"God's truth."

"Oh, then thanks. What do I do with it?"

"I've no idea."

"You've no idea what it's for or how it's used?"

"I've heard of one use for it."

"Go on then."

"There's an active volcano somewhere in Indonesia called the Merapi. And if starts to erupt, there's a big city somewhere nearby, and the local holy man goes to a special place, somewhere between the volcano and the city …"

"And he threatens the volcano?"

"He says some prayers and then plants the knife into the mountainside, so as to protect the city."

"You are sure this not another joke?"

"God's truth", he repeated, "so far neither the lava nor the burning smoke have ever arrived at the city."

"You keep saying that, 'God's truth'."

"Aye, I promise you it's true."

"Anyway, it's a very pretty object, thanks."

"Wait, as for prettiness, there is a 'piece de resistance'."

He went back into his bag and very carefully brought out something that was impossible to guess by its shape, the packaging was so heavy and voluminous.

"Y' be very careful wi' this."

I put it down on the floor and went to the kitchen to get a sharp knife. Sometimes the safest way to open up something is to have the means to cut firmly and quickly into it.

It took quite some minutes to finally get all the wrappings off of it.

It really was something special. It was a carved head and shoulders of an oriental type woman, in polished wood, and it truly was beautifully done.

"Why Duncan, it's beautiful," I was quite touched, "but it must have cost a fortune."

"Actually no", he smiled the smile of a canny Scot that had just found a two for one coupon for his favourite whiskey.

"It comes from a small village in Bali, where they do nothing else, and everything's dirt cheap."

Suddenly something switched on in my little brain.

"Is there anything else there that is special or very cheap?"

"Not really," he shook his head, "maybe the Batik. "

"What's a Batik?"

"It's not a thing, it's a process of dyeing material."

"Oh, that doesn't sound particularly interesting", my excitement waning.

"It's a very special process, using wax, or something, but Indonesia is world famous for it."

"World famous, so it's some sort of very expensive, secret process?"

"Na, you can buy Batik material there for next to nothing, this lungi, it's Batik."

"Duncan, you know how we three have always dreamt of starting something together?"

"Sure."

"Are you still interested?"

"Ye' but what?"

"Importing Indonesian goods, carved statues, Batik, stuff. If these are so cheap there, even covering transport and taxes, we could still make a killing."

"And we would be supporting native producers."

"Exactly," of course, I didn't give a shit for the native producers, I just needed to find a way to get rich, and as quickly as possible.

My future wife and present child were waiting for me to become a millionaire.

The young, noble, handsome and brave knight was off to kill Smaug, the expression of my incompetences and return.

The with the wonderous treasure from under the mountain, or over the waters, what-ever, to claim my princess bride.

"We, my transvestite friend with the hairy Scottish legs, are about to become rich.

You need to call Mike and get him to come down here. While I am to Max Bialystock, but not in little, old lady land, but big, fat, J.J. land'.

'Spring time for Duncan, for Mike and me ....'

## 10. Indian Tea and China Mugs

They were settled in the tiny, nurse's office. She had cleared off the little Formica topped table, and they were sitting in front of two steaming mugs of Tetley tea.

"I don't understand, how can a tuning fork make him react, while nothing else does?"

"Because it activities an energy centre, which is even deeper than the reactions to light and to touch."

"Biscuit?"

"That would be very kind of you, I am very much liking English biscuits," he takes one from the Noddy tin, opened in front of him.

"What do you mean, 'energy centre'? It sounds like there are mini power stations, hidden in parts of the body."

"Exactly, you are a very clever woman."

"Oh," she stops drinking her tea, "that's really kind."

"These energy centres are call the Chakras."

"I've heard of them, they've got be clean or they don't work right, and people get sick."

"That's more or less, it. We have seven major energy centres, Chakras.

And the better that they are functioning, and the more that they are lined up, then the more, healthy energy they can bring to each function."

"Function?"

"There are seven major chakras, The first one is called Muladhara meaning root support, the root or base chakra.

It is located here," he gets up and points to his behind, "At the base of the spine, what I am hearing is called the coccyx.

This is the chakra, which is linked to the concept of survival.

The next one, here, in the ummm sacr.., sac ....?"

"Sacrum?"

"Yes, yes there, it is called Svadhishthana, 'your own base' or sacral centre, that one deals with sexuality and pleasure.

Then there is Manipura, the 'city jewel', here in the belly-button, or ... solar plexus, it is also known as the hara.

This is the centre of power, and has links to confidence and self-esteem. Am I being boring?"

She has started to fidget slightly.

"No, no, not at all, it's, it's just, it's time that I have to make my rounds."

"Then, please go and do your job, I will go down to my new car, and bring up the bowls."

Her first reaction is to stop, and to ask …

"Please go, I'll explain later."

And so they both get up and leave the tiny office.

## 11.More Dealing with the Devil

Strangely enough, or so it seemed to me at the time, my father was particularly open to my business project.

"Well James, it seems to have potential as an idea, when do you plan to go an' check it out?"

"As soon as I find a way to finance a trip for the three of us."

"That shouldn't be too difficult."

"Could you finance us?"

"Nay bother", this was too easy, so I thought to risk the coup de grace.

"But after that, it might cost a lot to set up some sort of organised production over there; transport, taxes, warehousing, offices, publicity."

He smiled at me!

Was he mocking me for have the audacity to expect him to finance this?

"I see that your time at college was not totally wasted."

It irked me that he referred to my Alma Mata as a college, but somewhere there was a compliment buried under there.

"You can draw me up some sort of business plan, when you get back home.

Be in my office at two tomorrow afternoon, don't be later. Now I've work to do", and with that he got up and left the room.

I was in a daze, I was optimistic that he would help out a bit, but it seemed that he was ready to finance the whole of the operation.

Duncan was less optimistic, and more than that, he wasn't comfortable with J.J. financing everything, even if he would.

This was fortunate because J.J. was of the same mind…

I arrived at the office at five minutes to.

As soon as I announced myself to his secretary, I was immediately ushered in.

I was surprised to see that he wasn't alone, his solicitor, Baron Charles Holborn was seating himself discretely on a comfortable chair under one of the big open windows.

I politely nodded a greeting in his direction, he responded in kind.

"Well James, now it's time for you start your real path to becoming a man."

I waited silently for him to continue, "this is for you", he slid a small, white envelope towards me.

"What is it?"

"Why don't you open it? That would be a way to find out".

I advanced towards the desk and picked up the envelope.

It was the type that one might use for an invitation, in fact it was also the exact size of a credit card, a platinum American Express card.

A platinum American Express card with Pierre-Alain James Ferguson printed on it.

"This is for me?" It was like every Christmas, Easter and birthday all rolled into one.

"It's no use for anyone else."

"How, how, how can I thank you?"

"By signing this," he pushed a small pile of papers towards me.

"What is it?"

"It is an agreement between us that I am financing this little venture of yours under various conditions.

And this", he pointed to a different pile, "is for you to have access to my account, on which that credit card draws its cash.

That will be your business account, for which I stand surety for your line of credit."

"Oh," I was a little taken aback, but then what the hell?

"Where do I sign?"

"Not so fast laddie, there are some details that you need t' be clear about."

"Like what?"

"First and foremost, the other two must match whatever I advance."

"But Mike has no money, he can never match us."

"Together, Mike and Duncan together have to match my money."

"Okay, what else?"

"To be fair to your brother," the little traitor, "I canna give you the money.

I can only secure the finance for the project and that the money remains technically mine."

"And what does that change?"

"That I haven't given you an open cheque but not Jean Jacques."

"You can give him one as well, if you want."

"But I don't," he smiled over at me, "so if you still want to keep your shiny, new card …", he offered me his Montblanc.

The white stylised six-pointed star clearly picked out from the ebony black base.

I took the pen, and without another moment's reflexion, signed the documents.

He had had them printed out in triplicate, to be signed by both of us and witnessed by Holborn.

Mike had arrived by the time that I got back and was very excited by all the news.

However he became very red and uncomfortable when I explained about the fifty-fifty part of the deal.

But Duncan jumped in and promised that with the support of his family he could finance their contribution and that Mike would only need to find a symbolic sum of money so as to participate.

After that he cheered up and was already thinking how he could convince his local bank manager to give him a substantial loan based on the wonderful financial project that he had already started to create in his very active, but twisted little mind.

In the end we agreed that Duncan and I should each own 40 percent of the company each, with the remaining 20 percent shares in Mike's stubby, trembling hands.

So we were all set, next stop Indonesia.

## 12. English Tea and Tibetan Bowls

He is carrying in a quite heavy box, a blue and white box, adorned with a bunch of bananas on each corner, and on the lid. Blazed in blue, one can read the legend, 'Best Bio Bananas', and elegantly in black, 'Equitable Commerce'.

"What you got there?"

"These are singing bowls."

Is it like some sort of magic trick?"

"Yes, it is some sort of magic."

"Will you show me?"

"I would be most happy to be showing you."

"But first I need another tea, I sort of interrupted my break and your explanations."

"You are wanting that I continue to talk about the chakras?"

"I'll just make us another cuppa."

...........

"Then there is Anahata, 'unstruck', it is the heart chakra."

"And is found near the heart, and is something to do with loving?"

"Yes, yes that is right.

"Then there is the throat chakra, which is called Vishuddha and means 'especially pure', it is about the expression of emotions.

Then the Ajna centre, which means, 'command', but is also called the third-eye chakra, because it is here, just between and above the eyes."

"That was the one that you touched with the tuning fork."

"Yes, that was the one, it is about clear seeing, or what you might call, intuition.

Finally, there is the Crown chakra, which is at the top of the head."

"The fontanelle."

"Err, yes, there, there at the top. It is named Sahasrara, for the thousand-petaled lotus. It is about the state of pure consciousness."

"And what is all that got to do with Mr. Ferguson, who is in a highly comatose state?"

"But that is just it, I do not believe that Mr. Ferguson is really in a highly comatose state, I believe that Mr. Ferguson is suffering from the deepest of deep depressions."

"Are you serious?" She almost spills the tea, with the force of her response.

"I am not a doctor, so I cannot cure a coma, I don't know if anyone can."

"But you think that you can cure someone, that's so depressed that they don't want to wake up from a coma?"

Again, the strong feeling that she was dealing with a real 'nutta', resurfaced.

"I believe that there is a chance that I might help him wish to choose to regain consciousness."

"And just exactly how do you plan to do that?"

"With these, of course," and with that, he gestures towards the box.

"What, you gonna cure him with bananas?"

"No, there are no longer any bananas in this box."

Not, understanding the humour of the intentional mistake, he takes off the lid and takes out a small copper bowl.

"Don't you remember that I was saying that I have to get my bowls out of my new mini car?"

"Oh, yeh, the mini car. It's quite a big deal for you, ain't it?"

"It is very nice, and very kind of my benefactor to buy for me, my very own car, it's not a Ferrari, but it is very nice, just the same.

However, we are not talking here of cars, I am showing you some singing bowls, or standing bells, as they are sometimes called."

"But what can a bowl do to make someone wake up?"

"I have tested your patient and I am finding that each and every one of his chakra are blocked and unaligned.

This has surely happened because his life has led him away from his true centre."

"And so what do you plan to do?"

"I will help him to clear and realign his chakras, then he will wish to return."

And that little bowl will magically sort out all that?"

"I have seven bowls, each one is tuned into a chakra, I will place each one in turn on the chakra point, then I will make the bowl sing, and chant and also I will be talking to him."

"And that will heal him?"

"No."

"No?"

"He can only heal himself, I can be a sort of a guide."

"This, I will have to see."

"Then I will begin the first session."

## 13. Flying High

It was only once in the aeroplane, on the tarmac of London Heathrow, that, an almost forgotten neuron on a particular memory strip lit up.

Only then did I have the time and the space to reflect on what I'd done.

It seemed clear enough at the moment when the idea had came to me.

I had no pictures of Aideen, and I thought to hire someone to take some. After all, I now had almost unlimited funds.

And who else better skilled to do this little task, why, a private detective, of course.

The problem came out of his innocent question, 'is that all that you want me to do?'

His reflection was, that if I wanted some pictures of this child, it would cost hardly anything more to keep an eye on the mother, and photograph anything, 'interesting'.

'Why not?' And there you have it, the deal was done.

I hadn't honestly thought too much about it in that moment, but, now, after all the running, organising and stress to get us off the ground and heading in the right direction, it occurred to me that I had set a private eye to spy on Angelique, and to photograph anything, 'interesting'.

It was an unwarranted invasion of her privacy, she'd done nothing to deserve that, I should call the 'dick' and get him to just take the photos, as soon as we land, that's what I'll do.'

Or so I intended at the time, I really did.

Of course by the time we arrived, I'd totally forgotten about all that, what with the tiredness and then everything else that happened, it just slipped out of my mind.

We had left Heathrow at 10:50 and we arrived the next day at 07:40, only 25 minutes later than on the planning.

The flight was supposed to be about 14 hours, but they are also 8 hours ahead of us, I couldn't work out the math, and certainly aren't going to bother now.

We were a little concerned about the connecting flight, and had given ourselves over 2 hours to make the conection, but were not sure how it would work out.

Duncan had come directly from Malaysia, where he had stayed a few days to see some of the sites.

We needn't have worried, we were directed directly towards the Indonesian departure lounge, no need to check our passports or anything.

And our bags would be transferred without our having to intervene at all.

It happened in a kind of oneiric trance, we floated through the airport, and then, without any clear intervention from our part, we were on a flight to Jakarta.

From that stop, we took the 12:20 flight, and, right on time arrived at the tiny terminal at Yogyakarta.

Why Yogyakarta? (Pronounced Jaja-kata, for your edification), one might ask?

We had spent quite a lot of time and money, (no internet then!), researching, phoning and reflecting on what to do with the Batik part of the project.

J.J. had even put in his 10 penny worth, (after all it was his money that was funding half of it), and eventually we all agreed that the best way to guarantee production and delivery was to build a factory.

Unfortunately it was not possible to build one on Bali, as it is relatively small and it would spoil the touristic experience to build a factory there.

As we needed to secure a solid transport system, it was clear that the factory needed to be near an airport.

Of course we next thought of Jakarta, but it was already very industrialised, the locals had plenty of other work opportunities and we would have to build quite out of town and the traffic into the city and towards the airport would also not be optimal.

It was Duncan that suggested Yogyakarta, it was the 2$^{nd}$ city of Indonesia, but as yet very little industrialised, however, it did have its very own airport.

So that is how we came to be landing in Yogyakarta, just after lunch time.

Yogyakarta can be hot, sometimes hot and dry, sometimes hot and humid, but mostly hot.

Duncan wasted no time digging out his lungi, but neither Mike nor I cared to join the locals in that attire.

Actually, the height of fashion was to be wearing Levi jeans, the young and the hip, were into western culture, as much as they could and as much as they could afford.

They must have been sweating like pigs!

I had had the good sense to have brought with me very light, almost cheese cloth, trousers, thank God, a bit chilly in London, but perfect for here.

We took a sort of taxi or rickshaw to the hotel we had booked, not knowing much about the local habits, (Duncan should have known!), we must have paid about 10 times the correct fare.

Not that it translated that much into pounds, but I'm not used to being ripped off, and I didn't appreciate that after having travelled for what seemed like days, our first welcome was to robbed by the local cab company.

Of course it happens all over the world, even in the UK, but doesn't make it any less painful.

So we installed ourselves in our hotel, everything seemed quite correct, except of course there was no international telephone service.

We had to walk down to the post office and book an international call, if we wished to phone the UK.

We had arrived just a little too soon for easy international calling or many years before decent portable phone use.

Then there was the washing facilities, as this was quite an expensive and posh hotel, it did at least have a normal toilet, (Mike had checked on that).

What he hadn't thought to ask about was the bathing or showering system.

They had this very beautifully tiled water reservoir, which we filled from a hosepipe, from there we were expected to take a type of big ladle, scoop up the water and douse ourselves like that.

After getting over the shock, the truth was it was really okay as a system, and we all got quickly used to it.

As a weird twist of fate or happenstance, the volcano that Duncan had talked about that was magically stopped by the sacred Kris knife, was our close neighbour and the city that was protected was none other than Yogyakarta, some joke eh?

As Duncan was supposed to know his way around in this country, we let him make the first contacts with the officials of the area, but he kept finding himself bogged down by red tape.

Each time he thought that he had something organised, one official after another would shrug his shoulders and say that he was missing some special paper that was lacking.

It was only after some time that I got to talk to the interpreter alone that it became clear that the special paper that was lacking, was the folding sort.

It was normal in this country that everything that you wanted to get legalised, stamped or approved, cost between 10 – 20 percent more as back shish, for the person giving the authorisation.

Duncan being as honest as the day, straight as an arrow and in some things, thick as a brick, had totally missed these messages and had passed his days hitting one brick wall after another.

It only took me a couple of hours to get everything sorted out, and within a week, we had the official permission to create our factory.

As a celebration, we first asked to be taken to the most expensive and hip restaurant in town.

To our surprise we ended up in the commercial centre, modern and air-conditioned, looking at a miserable Macdonald's franchise.

Fortunately there was also an excellent coffee house also in the centre, which served some wonderful, house specialities.

From there we took ourselves to a temple compound, just a few miles outside of Yogyakarta, to a place known as Prambanan to see the Javanese Ramayana dance-drama, (or so it is described in the guide books.)

It was a big open air event, with fiery torches all around the arena, which is really what it was, a big space, flattened and covered with sand, I think.

They were 'dancing' some religious text, which neither Mike nor I were interested to hear about, so Duncan contented himself to become enlightened without our participation.

I must say that the dance was quite breath-taking, the women incredibly fine and beautiful and the costumes exceptional.

The dancing, although not one of my usual cultural activities, was also really well done, although I must admit, it did seem to drag on a bit after a while and I started to feel rather bored.

It was only by fantasising how it would be to have the girls, semi or totally naked, dancing over me, that kept me from leaving and letting the others take a taxi home without me.

Things started advancing well and Duncan had finally understood the concept of a type of extra but unofficial tax that had to paid, so we were ready to pass over to our second port of call.

Only, before he would let us leave, he insisted that we all visited some old Buddhist temples.

All arguments that he was the one that would be coming back often and hence would have more than ample time to build a second home right next door to them, fell on deaf ears.

At was an experience that he wanted to share with us, and share it, he would.

So we did, we booked a standard tour, that way we wouldn't get more ripped off them all the other tourists.

We crammed ourselves into a stinky, old bus and suffered the 25 or so miles to the temples.

Yes, it was quite an impressive site, a cross between a Buddhist temple and an Egyptian pyramid.

Duncan said that we should go in a certain gate and walk round in a certain direction, and on the walls were really interesting things inscribed.

This particular pilgrimage I managed to convince him to do another time, and with a sigh of a disheartened Mr Chips, faced with a class of philistines, or would that be more John Alderton and the class of 5C, he allowed us out before the final school bell.

From there we took taxis and ferries to Bali, and soon arrived in the village of Ubud.

It was quite an ordinary village as far as I was concerned, but what made it interesting for us was the little village named Mas, about 15 miles away.

Mas is a village of wood carvers; there are literally dozens of them and they are all of pretty high standard.

I started the day we were to go there in pretty high spirits, but when we got there, I was faced with a certain frustration.

Any possibility to bid down their prices, even offering to buy fixed and regular quantities of their work, was of little avail.

I suppose, that after the usual bargaining that most savvy customers know about, there is little enough benefit for all the hours of work, for them to be able to go much further down.

It still didn't help my mood, I felt a bit humiliated in front of the others, until Mike cheered me up.

He wrote up a rough projection of the profits that we could make, even at the 'regular' prices, once we had shipped them and marked them up at a decent price, it was in the order of 5 times our outlay.

I finished the day in higher spirits, I had bought almost everything that they had finished.

Then I got Mike to come and tell me, loudly that he had done the calculations and they were too dear, and not to buy them.

I argued back at him that I had almost finished the deal and that I was about to buy all the stock.

Mike threw up his hands in a rather too theatrical gesture for me, but seemed convincing for the villagers.

So when I shrugged my shoulders to them and started walking away … 'nuf to say, we finished off with an extra, one off, none repeatable, special blue moon price of 10% off.

Duncan didn't seem amused, but Mike and I knew that we had made a coup, and we were deservedly proud of it.

He just looked at us, counting our pieces of silver, even before we had cached in our wooden chips.

"Come on Duncan, I'll take you to somewhere that will made you feel better".

"Ya had no need to do that, we would ha' made a good profit even without screwing the poor beggars out of their deserved benefits."

"Next time it'll be you that deals with them, we'll be back in the UK screwing the customers", I smirked back at him.

He just tuttered, like an angry grandmother.

"Come on, let's go".

"Where are you taking me now?"

"Somewhere that you'll like, promise".

Fortunately, I'd overheard some other tourists talking about a special temples not so far away.

And knowing what Duncan would have a liking for, I'd informed myself of the details.

It turned out to be a monkey forest, actually, a Sacred Monkey Forest Sanctuary, (Guide book capitalisation, not mine).

And there were over 500 irritating, scratching, biting, little devils of monkeys, at any time.

Somewhere in the forest there were several temples including a "Holy Spring" bathing temple and another temple used for cremation ceremonies.

Other than buying a small selection of other local goods; Kris's, masks etc., there was little else to do than pack the crates for shipping back to the UK.

Then making sure that all the forms were correctly signed and that everyone that needed their palms oiling, were duly oiled, we packed our own luggage and return back home.

Returning home, I was confronted with the error of asking the private dick to 'keep an eye on Angelique.'

## 14.Healing from the Himalayas

He has brought his banana box into the hospital room, and she has uncovered the patient.

Leaving him looking rather miserable and vulnerable in his skimpy, hospital gown.

Out of the box, she discovers the seven bronze bowls, the last one out must have a rim diameter of about 12 inches, the size of an old vinyl LP disk.

"You be careful with that," she warns him, as she realises that that large and obviously heavy object is to be placed, just below her patient's private parts.

"Don't be worrying, I have done this before."

And so saying so, he gently and carefully, places the bowl on the patient. He then takes out a packet of sandalwood incense, and an incense holder.

"We begin?"

"Sure, I've just done my rounds,
everything should be okay for a while."

He goes and closes the door, lights
several incense sticks and begins to wave
them about. He then starts to chant.

"Teyata Om Bekanze Mahabekanze
Bekanze Radza Samutgate Soha"

After several minutes of chanting he
begins to softly tap the bowl with a small,
decorated, wooden stick.

The deep sound and low vibration can be
felt in the stomach and below.

He then ceases to chant, but continues to
sound the bowl.

"You are existing in space, where all that
you can be experiencing is fog or mist, or
something like that."

"You might believe that you are in hell, but you are not, Faron."

The nurse gives a quizzical look at the use of a name that does not exist on her charts. The monk just smiles back at her.

"You cannot know who I am, or what or even where I am, but I am here to help you."

"You are not dead, you are in an in-between place, in-between, here and there."

"It is not purgatory, however, you might choose to call it that."

"Where you should go next, will have to be decided."

"You have now, the possibility to change.

We know that you cannot to change what you have done, in the past. However, you can change who you are now."

"And even if you fear that it is being too late."

"It is never too late, or else there would be no point in you being here."

"So now you have the choice, to advance, or to continue to stay here, in this no place."

"And to stay here, for as long as takes for you to accept to change."

"It can only be your choice, change or stay," he smiles at her.

"It is the only choice, to change, or stay the same."

"So, to change or remain the same?"

Suddenly the body spasms.

"Okay, change it is."

"Change it is,"      the nurse
repeats.

"Okay,"      affirms the
monk.

## 12. Dealing with a Dick

He wasted no time in contacting me, as soon as I signalled my presence back in the UK.

"Mr. Ferguson, I've got some very interesting photographs to share with you."

It was like a dog who had just dug up an old filthy bone, and was carrying it towards you.

If he had one, I'm sure that he would be wagging his tail, like a sapling in a storm.

It didn't take a mind reader to guess that the photos were not of Aideen.

"She's got herself a boyfriend, the little slut."

"Give me the photos, and the negatives, take your money and get out."

I really wanted to hit him, who the Hell did he think that he was to call her a slut?

A two bit, peeping Tom shit, to think to cast aspersions on her.

"It's 200 pounds."

"Send me the bill."

"It's cash on delivery."

"Then sue me."

"Give me back the photographs, they're not paid for yet."

"Do you know where the nearest hospital emergency room is?"

"What?"

" 'Cus you'll be visiting it shortly if you don't get out of my way, …., and," (another thought suddenly crossed my mind), "if you speak of this to anyone or if anyone sees these photographs, my family has many contacts with the authorities.

That would be a professional breach of confidence and you'll never work in this country again!"

"If you don't pay me."

"It's because you haven't sent me a bill.

And if you only work cash in hand to avoid paying taxes, I'm sure that the Inland Revenue would have the time to help you control your accounts."

"I'll send you a bill."

"With all of the negatives."

I'm sure that he swore under his breath as he left, but I was much too angry to worry about him now.

Looking back, it is difficult to really understand my reactions, (reactions plural), because there were several, and they were mixed.

I was, it was true, shocked, angry and sorry to admit, jealous that she was seeing somebody.

I wanted to lash out at her, the feelings of abandon and betrayal again surfaced.

I wanted to hurt her, to hurt him, to break this up, which of course I eventually did.

But at the same time, and this is where it becomes so much more complicated for me.

I was outraged that he had followed her.

I was outraged that he had spied on her, taken photographs, stolen into her private, intimate life.

And that he would dare, in my presence, to have the gall to call her a slut, it was all that I could do not to beat the very shit out of him then and there.

I don't know if every human's psyche is as complex and twisted as mine, but, even now, I have trouble accepting to have had such strong and contradictory emotions, at exactly the same time.

The new boyfriend, whose name I don't even remember, if I even did know his name, was a young guy who lived in the village and worked in the factory.

I paid a criminal type from London to pay him a visit, claiming to be an associate of a member of one of the Southern mafia families.

He warned the guy that Aideen was the daughter of the mobster, and even if he didn't have time to visit Angelique often, he still considered her his property, and would not act kindly to anyone that encroached on his territory.

He also warned him to tell no-one of this information, for his friend was trying to protect Aideen, his daughter, and if other mafia families found out it would make him vulnerable.

For some unclear reason, suddenly, the guy found Angelique less attractive, and the relationship petered out.

I cannot say that I felt particularly proud to have orchestrated this little piece of theatre, but I couldn't not do it either.

## 13. On the Up

The marketing of our products was to be double; we would be wholesale importers, but we would also aim to open a number of retail outlets.

All in all it took a year to get everything in place in the UK, it took two years to get the factory up and functioning in Yogyakarta.

Eventually we had all the pieces of the puzzle in place; a working factory producing Batik material, access to the carved statues in Mas, one or two friendly suppliers of other Indonesian artefacts, at reasonable prices.

We had also rented a warehouse, cum sales room in the London Docklands, and finally, a quite big retail outlet on Southwark St., (being the closest to central London that we could find a afford).

The opening was going to be quite a big affair, and we had issued invitations left, right and centre.

As this was something that Maman really enjoyed doing, J.J. pressured us to allow her to get involved.

As she had always been open and friendly, (abate, in a particularly distant manner), to both Duncan and Mike, (guests should always be well treated), welcoming them when-ever and as often as they might fancy to visit, they could find no reason to object.

So in the end, much against my better judgment, I acquiesced and so, Antoinette-Marie Claude Armitage Ferguson became the head of the BIFTA (British – Indonesian Fair Trading Association), launch committee.

(By the way, no surprises, it was basically Duncan that had come up with the name.

Although I had insisted to add the term, 'Association' even though technically it was totally incorrect, it just sounded good with the fair trade bit).

We had succeeded to get some pretty good publicity about the fair trade angle, many in the more left wing rags, and some of the wood sculptures had been featured in some high end magazines.

I should have been more involved in the big launch, but my head, (and heart), were attracted elsewhere.

After having returned after our visit to Indonesia, it was only logical that I should re-install myself back into the house, as my main place of residence.

Jean Jacques was now rarely there, he had finished his law degree and had found a trainee position with J.J.'s own solicitors; Smiley, Withers & Holborn.

With them, he had commenced his stage of LPC (Legal Practice Course).

When he did find himself at home, and in my presence, he gave a respectful nod of acknowledgement and left me well alone.

It is true, after so much time, years, my determination to never speak to him again was starting to waiver.

And when both J.J and Maman, begged me to allow him to attend the opening of the store, I ceded without too much resistance.

But more than that, spending time in and around the village, meant that there was ample opportunity to bump into both Angelique and Aideen.

It would have been more noticeable than not if we were to avoid or ignore each other.

So after a moment of uncertainty, we chose to act as if we were old acquaintances, that had known each other years back, but had nothing much to do with each other now.

This was in no way discussed or decided between us, it just became to happen naturally.

I was a little anxious the first time that we crossed Angelique in the pub, she was with some of my old school friends, I was with J.J.

"Pierre-Alain, over here", I threw a glance over at my father, who returned the question with non-committal shrug.

So I went over to the group.

"Hi guys, how's everyone doing? Hi Angelique, how you doing? How's the kid?"

"I'm fine, Aideen is doing fine, and you?"

"Oh I'm working towards becoming a millionaire."

"Well, you can buy us all a round when you do." Someone laughed back at me.

And so that was it, J.J. made no comment on our, (Angelique's and mine), exchange, and that was enough of a seal of approval for me.

That was pretty much okay, my anger against Angelique was also cooling down, what wasn't cooling down was my desire to have contact with Aideen.

Aideen was seven at this time, she was as pretty as her mother, but with a bit of me thrown in.

Of course she knew who I was, it was a small village and everyone knew everyone else, and I was not that unremarkable either.

When I would meet her with Angelique, she would make a little curtsey and repeat, "bonjour monsieur Pierre- Alain".

The first time it really shook me, then I noticed the slight curl on the lips of Angelique, and so decided not to react inappropriately.

« Bonjour Aideen, comment vas-tu?" She looked lost and confused.

"Elle va très bien, merci", her mother rescued her. "We still have a little more to learn my peach. Bonne journée, Pierre-Alain."

"Bye Angelique," and then they were gone.

And so Aideen came to know me as an unimportant, old friend of her mother's, who lived in the big house and who spoke French, like her mother could.

These passing moments of contact became like a drug, and I might find myself, walking towards the little school, just before recreation time, like some old paedophile pervert, just to catch a peek of her.

I returned to London in style, J.J. driving his vintage Bentley, I sat in the front with him, Maman and Jay, took the back seats.

I do have to say, even if somewhere it pains me terribly, Maman had done a fantastic job on the launch; she had managed to organize Indonesian food, music and dancers.

There was also a lot of press, many dealing with houses and furnishings; Ideal Home, Good Housekeeping, Country Life and Homes & Gardens.

Then there were the glosses;
Cosmopolitan, Elle, Marie Claire, etc.,
etc.

Not only had she organized all that, but
she also, of course, invited some rather
interesting people.

"Pierre-Alain, could you please take a
moment of valuable time, to say hello to
someone?"

It difficult to imagine that she could be
referring to me.

I turned round to see her leading a very
fashionably dressed, (or say I guessed – I
don't know the first thing about fashion),
middle-aged dowager.

She was short, overweight, with a very
complicated hairstyle.

Maybe the idea was that people would have their attention drawn to the hair, so not to notice just how ugly the face under it really was.

I have never seen anyone bothering to play at putting heavy women's makeup on a pit-bull, now, looking at this specimen of womanhood, I could surely understand why.

"Pierre-Alain, I would like to introduce you to Ms. Vera Armstrong Jones."

"Bonjour Madame, quel plaisir. How can be of assistance?"

"Ms. Vera Armstrong Jones is the head buyer for Liberty's store on Regent St.

As if I wouldn't know where Liberty's store was, it is almost next door to Hamley's Toy Shop, every child's Aladdin's cave, even if they've now moved it one shop down.

"And how might I be of service to Liberty's of Regent St?"

"Ms Vera …." She then cut my mother off.

"We would be rather interested in the possibility of creating a unique line of Batik designs, although, as I understand it, in the traditional Javanese language, it is also known as Kain meaning fabric."

"Quite right you are, Madam …" Duncan had somewhere sensed that I might be in difficulty and had come quickly to rescue me.

"Ms. Vera Armstrong Jones." I presented her to him.

"You have certainly done your homework, I am Duncan McCloud, and I am the Indonesian liaison member of the team.

May I show you some of the beautiful designs that we are having fabricated at this very moment.

Of course, having our own factory, allows us full control on all aspects of the production process."

And off they went.

"Soyez un peu plus discret, s'il vous plait", but, just the same, I could see that she was particularly pleased with both of us.

I passed the evening in a dream of success; every birthday, confirmation, bar-mitzvah, First Rice, Krypteia and graduation all rolled into one.

I was drunk with happiness and with success, I even looked round to find Jay, to share my good humour with him.

But it seemed that some-time during the evening, he had developed a migraine and had discretely called a taxi and retired back to the 'London flat'.

Being on so much of a high, when the last of the guests had finally finished all that they could eat and drink, and had buggered off, it was unthinkable to think of going home to bed.

So we found ourselves an after-hours club, and carried on drinking and celebrating until morning.

When I finally dragged myself out of bed, sometime in the late afternoon, I found myself alone in the flat, they had all gotten up earlier, and had abandoned me to return home to New Chapel.

Not that I particularly cared, I was now a success, it wouldn't take that long to build up my fortune, and then return to claim my flaming prize.

But the best laid plans of mice and men …

## 14. Tea & Toast

It had been some weeks since the monk had begun to work on the un-waking man.

Of course there were other nurses on the night shift during that time, but, as chance would have it, tonight she was back on duty.

"Please, is it okay that I am coming into your office?"

"Hello, have you already finished for tonight?"

"I would very much like to ask you to make us both a cup of tea."

"Why, is there something to celebrate?"

"Yes."

"Your employer has bought you a Ferrari?"

"Better than that?"

"Better than a Ferrari?"

"He has moved."

"Who has moved? Moved where?"

"He, he, him, Ferguson. He has moved."

"E's waking up, Oh God, I'll have to call the duty doctor."

"No, no, no, he is not yet waking up, oh no, no, no. That is not to be for some time … if ever."

"What do you mean, 'if ever'? I thought that you were going to do some miracle stuff with your singing bowls, and then he was going to wake up."

"It is true, that that is what hopefully will be going to happen."

"But?"

"But I have been thinking, and things are not being always so straight forwards."

"What things are not so straight forward?"

"You see, all his chakra, are very messed up."

"And your talking and chanting and sticking the bowls on him, are going to sort them out?"

"Exactly."

"Don't see the problem here."

"You see, everybody comes into this world with the chakras messed up."

"But you said that his problem was his chakras."

"Yes, all his charkas are in a very bad way.

But every person that comes into this world has work to do on the level of their chakras.

That is one expression of their karma, working through your karma, is the same thing as harmonising your chakras."

"So my chakras are also messed up?"

"But not anywhere nearly as his are."

"So, where's the problem?"

"If one believes that our challenges in life, are reflected in the state of our chakras.

And so, our life's purpose is to purify, harmonise and align our chakras."

"So, here's your tea, if all the chakras are sorted, then there is nothing else to do, then what next?"

"Exactly, you are hitting the nail directly on the head. If there is no more karma to heal, why come back?"

"So, if you do your job right, he might just choose to not wake up, but to die?"

"That would be being correct."

"Then, just don't do it right, only sort out the chakras enough for him to wake up."

"That, I cannot do. Already, what I am doing is not really controlled.

I have to keep meditating and talking and singing and sounding the bowls. And then, if a miracle happens, I move onto the next chakra."

"And did that happen?"

"Yes, yes it did. Just now. Just now I sounded the bowl, and his breathe resonated with the vibration.

I thought that maybe I was mistaken, or that I was dreaming, but I did it again, and again, and again. His base chakra is clear and aligned."

"I'll drink to that."

And so they toasted the victory with tea.

## 15. The End of the Rainbow

We had all the right ingredients to become rich; a quasi-monopoly on goods or services that were in demand and of which we could force a ridiculously high margin.

Or so I thought.

Duncan was to become a royal pain in the arse, thorn in my side and hole in my bucket!

His bloody Christian background kept getting in the way of us earning the grotesquely, unreasonable profits that we should.

Firstly he quibbled about the prices we were asking for the goods themselves.

"It's much too high, we're robbing folk, they don't know how little it costs us to buy and ship this stuff."

"It's called making a profit."

"No, James, it's called ripping people off."

"We are providing a service, we source merchandise, that most have no way to find or t' buy.

Then we negotiate to purchase the goods, then we organise for them to get shipped out, no easy matter, as well you know.

That we see to shipping, the landing, the importation paperwork, fees and taxes, then we transport them to the warehouse and then to here, in this shop that we rent at crook rates.

And then we or one of the pretty assistants helps the client to choose, just the right object for them.

And all that takes huge effort, resources, creativity and cash investment."

"I know just how a business works."

"Then you know that to pay back all the investment, on all levels, we need to make obscene profits, for at least a year or two."

"I'll have t' think on it," and off he went.

Fortunately the joint front of Mike and I, and the argument that we were responsible for this end quietened him down for a moment.

It was only when he started sending faxes asking for more money to be wired that we realised that he had now refocused his need for 'fairness' on the working conditions of our employees.

I took the first available flight and ended up in fight that would have ended up physical if Duncan had not decided to back down in the last minute.

I accepted a small wage increase on our initial wage agreements and gave Duncan a certain latitude on improving working conditions, but with a clearly defined and agreed budget.

Duncan's inability to screw both the workers and the clients was proving and eventually proved to be our undoing.

It was true that we were doing reasonably well, but we could have done much better.

We also had to face up to the realities with dealing with big, well established businesses.

They had been in business much longer than we had, and they had managed to survive and prosper using exactly the same formula that I was proposing; screw both the suppliers and the customers.

The problem with this, was that in their buying and selling model, we were the suppliers, hence, we were also there to get screwed by them.

For instance, the wonderful contact that my mother had orchestrated for us with Liberty's, proved to be more trouble than it was worth.

They were incredibly fussy about the designs, they had to be reproduced exactly to their model, each piece of fabric to be perfect and a guarantee that their designs would not be sold to anyone else, and all that at a very preferential price.

To have our Batik, sold in Liberty's, seemed to be the show case that we needed, so we agreed to all their terms.

But then they rejected half of the first batch, as not being up to standard.

At the same time reminding us that we were not allowed to sell the rejects to anyone else.

It was then that I realised what a 'crock of shit', I had bought myself by signing the contract with them.

Eventually I succeeded to convince them to take the 'seconds', which they could sell during their famous sales, at no more than it cost me to import.

Whether they had planned this all along, or not, I might never know, but it still leaves a sour taste in my mouth.

When, during a trip home, I complained loudly to my parents about the deal, my mother totally defended their treatment of me.

She responded, in English, (so that J.J, could fully understand and support her and because my French was becoming a bit rusty).

"What else could you expect from a store of their standing?

They have a reputation to uphold, if your factory cannot produce goods of good quality, why should your clients suffer to accept shoddy goods?"

"She's not wrong you know laddie, if my factories were to produce sub-standard parts, I'd soon be out of business."

Jean Jacques, who also happened to be present just looked up towards me and shrugged his shoulders.

The little, traitor worm, always sucking up to the parents, and to think that I was almost ready to forgive and forget.

So, the goose that was set to lay the golden eggs, only ended up producing sterling silver, something of quality and value, but nowhere near as interesting as promised.

We had been operating for three years
when trouble struck.

Duncan had shown himself once too
often to being weak and unconvinced
about the work conditions and wages and
the workers had sensed his vulnerability.

So they decided to go on strike.

Duncan was totally at a loss as what to
do, so again I had to make the long haul
flight, half way across the world.

When I got there, things had heated up,
so I had no alternative but to threaten that
either they went back to work
immediately or they would all be fired.

That was, here and now, without any
form of severance pay, nor even the
wages that was owed to them.

It seems that I went a bit too far.

It seemed that someone decided that if I was serious, then they would not be the only ones to suffer, and set fire to the factory.

The response of the workers was for me totally unexpected, they rallied round without a moment's hesitation, nor that much thought for their own safety.

The fire lit up the night sky, some people in the city were even convinced that the Merapi, the volcano was erupting and ran out screaming, causing some quite unnecessary addition stress.

We managed to save most of the factory's machinery but all the stock was of course ruined.

The workforce was again concerned for their livelihood, and this time it was my place to thank them for their efforts and to reassure then that we would rebuild the factory.

Also that I would find the means to offer a small wage rise and pay them their usual wages while we had the factory rebuilt.

I hated to think exactly what this financial setback would look like on the balance sheet, and that must have been the moment that I had decided that I was going to separate myself from Duncan.

You see, even if it was my threat that literally set off the spark that caused the fire, it was Duncan's uncertain management style that had dried the tinder.

All in all it took two years to set up the sale of our, (mine and Mike's), shares in the company.

Fortunately, with my 40 percent and Mike's 20, whoever would wish to buy us out, would buy themselves a controlling interest, and, for all intents and purposes own the company.

Of course I had to wait until the factory was rebuilt and profits were coming in again.

Mike had started some creative accounting, adding profits where there ought to have been, more than, where they actually were.

We covered much of this theoretical extra income by paying all three of us bonuses that didn't really exist.

We even bought out a small material shop, which theoretically, suddenly became an immensely successful retailer.

Selling vast quantities of our Batik, and generating the profits that Mike was happily inscribing into our books.

To cover ourselves, we had to dig into my private capital and he had to greatly increase his overdraft.

It was quite a long term scam, but we had to make the business as attractive as possible, to catch a big fish, you need a juicy bait.

At the end of a little over two years, all was ready.

We were generating very healthy profits, our books had been independently audited, we had even paid up the taxes on our supposed earnings.

Michael Singh was a second generation Pakistani immigrant.

His father had arrived here 35 years ago with nothing more than the clothes on his back and the need to survive.

He had done much, much better than that.

Through immense hard work, not only himself, but all the members of his continually growing family.

With that, and a certain Asian intelligence, he had succeeded to find himself, eventually, quite rich.

Michael was now looking to make himself his mark in the world, but he, different from his father, had a quite considerable sum of money to invest, and the garment industry interested and excited him.

He planned to buy the company and eventually turn it round into a high class clothes making enterprise.

We showed him the books from the last two years, and he was suitable impressed.

We showed him our offices, which also impressed him, we showed him the sales room with the attractive sales staff, and he was ready to buy.

When he inquired just why we were selling our shares, we simply stated that we were entrepreneurs and as the business was now functioning well, there was now little interest or challenge for us.

We were not particularly interested in growing it into some sort of empire, as it was the small scale and rarity that meant that we could sell at a premium, otherwise we would have to totally change our whole concept.

Simply, we were just wishing to cash in our chips, enjoy a hefty profit, and look towards new horizons.

Our story seemed feasible enough and we set about discussing the details of the sale.

At the same time, through some unforeseen bad luck and happenstance, the little retail store that had succeeded for the last two years to sell enormous quantities of our merchandise, experienced a terrible cash flow problem and closed its doors.

By the time that the deal was signed, sealed and delivered, the business was only 'earning' sixty percent of the last two years average, but as everyone knows, that's always the risk in any business.

After paying back the cash that we had 'invested' over the past two years, we calculated that we had made a fourfold profit on our initial investments.

Which meant that after I had paid my father back, and Mike had repaid his overdraft, we would walk out of this deal fairly rich men.

No, I hadn't become a millionaire, but I could at least show to my father that I was capable to earn real money.

And I now had more than enough to invest in any other business venture of my choosing.

I was looking forward to returning home and crowing, just a little, well actually, quite a lot.

"… and that is how I have managed to quadruple your investment in just a few years!"

I finished the whiskey, and thunked the empty glass back down on the chipped bar.

"So, how do you expect me to react to this story o' yours?"

"I trust that you will be pleased, proud and positive.

To know be convinced about my ability to take on the responsibilities of a husband and father."

He didn't answer straight away, just signed for Rick to refill our glasses.

That done, he turned slowly towards me.

"I'm sorry James, but that's not the way that a Ferguson functions," he said it in a very quiet, even sad tone.

"What do you mean? I made a killing."

"I thought that we had educated you better. We are neither crooks nor traitors, I have always been fair and honest, with everyone.

When I took over the works from Patrick, I didn't leave him out on the street, jobless, I took him back in.

I made him works manager, he even gets
a percentage of the profits as an annual
bonus.

I work on the Roman system, yes conquer
all that you can, but as soon as you have
the power, return it to those that ran
things before.

And let them return to doing their jobs,
but this time better, because now I make
the major decisions.

You left your supposed best friend
stranded on a lost island, with a new
major share-holder partner, without so
much as a fax.

And you cooked the books for two years,
preparing to swindle some poor, innocent
bugger out of his family's hard earned
cash."

"Well, I'm not going to give anything
back, not one penny.

I've worked for that money, and so help me, I'm going to keep it."

"Y' better take another shot at your scotch, 'cus you're not goin' to like what I'm going to say next."

"What?"

"I've frozen the bank account and blocked your card, it's been officially lost or stolen, so I'd advise you not to try and use it again, you might find yourself arrested on suspicion of theft or fraud."

"What?" I seemed to understand all the words, but the meaning was not gelling into any type of coherent sense.

"You have frozen my bank account? You've blocked my credit card?"

"Actually no."

I almost had time to breathe normally before, "both the bank account and credit card are mine.

I just allowed you access to them. Now that access has been rescinded, that's all."

"But I earned all that money, it has to be mine."

"Here, here's a copy of the contract that you signed. I don't suppose that you've ever taken the time t' read it."

"What am I supposed to have read?"

With several shots inside me, and the shock of this news, I was really having trouble seeing straight.

"This paragraph here," he pointed to it with his cigar.

The rather abrupt gesture, caused the accumulated head of ash to detach itself from the cigars' end and scatter itself all over the contract.

"What fucking paragraph?" I wrenched the paper from his other hand, shaking the grey powder off in a particularly violent way.

The pub had gone very quiet, all heads were turned towards me, some people were even quietly laughing.

"What are you laughing at? You're laughing at yourselves," I screamed at them.

Embarrassed, they quickly turned away, and returned to doing, doing whatever they were doing before.

"Here," J.J. gently took the papers from my shaking hands, "we'll discuss this tomorrow, when you're a little more sober."

"No, show me now, I'm okay." I managed to calm myself down a bit.

"It says here, that you have full access to the account, to invest the money as you should see fit, as my fully accredited representative."

"Representative? What do you mean representative?"

"As I said at the time, I canna' give you a blank cheque, and not Jean Jacques.

Which was to say, that I never gave you any money, it was always mine. That said, any profits that you succeeded to earn, are mine, all and only mine."

"But where's my share?" 'Where's Leo Bloom's share?' Echoed in my head.

"You don't have a share. You've lived very well these last few years, that's your wages.

Everything that you've bought, your posh car, expensive hi-fi, fashion clothes, those you've earned, those you keep.

But as for the cash in the bank, well now you've sold the business, you've no more need for that now."

"No more need? But I've earned for you a fortune."

I know that I was almost whimpering, but it was either that or smashing the glass on the counter and cutting his throat with the broken end.

"Yes you've earned quite well with it, I thought you'd lose it all, so that's nay bad.

But no, not a fortune, and I might well have earned even more with it, if I'd had your opportunities."

"But you're going to give me some of the profits, aren't you?

I need some money to buy a house for me and Angelique and Aideen."

"Y' haven't understood anything have you?

Pierre-Alain, I'm ashamed of you, and you certainly have shown nothing to prove that you're man enough to be responsible for a family.

You just leave them all alone, they're doing very well without you."

And with that he got up off of his stool, turned and left. He didn't even offer to drive me home, even if it was clear that I would refuse it anyway.

I turned back to the bar and ordered a double, then doubting that I had any cash to pay for it, I asked if I could put it on J.J.'s slate.

Rick had no problem with that so I just carried on drinking until I blanked out.

## 16. The Path towards Harmony

The weeks passed without much incident.

From time to time the monk and the nurse would meet, sometimes would drink tea together, even, there would be news.

"Another?"

"Yes, we are advancing. The work might seem slow, but we are passing up and up the chakras."

"So where are you now?"

"Now we are at the heart chakra."

"Well, that should be an easy one."

"You are thinking so?"

"Sure doesn't everyone love to be loved?"

"Feeling unloved is the greatest distress of all.

And when it becomes contaminated with feelings of loss, rejection, and hatred, and when we have no love, not even for ourselves, then this is the most difficult of all chakras to be healing."

"But you can do it, can't you?"

"I am fearing that I do not have enough love in me to open up his heart."

"So what are going to do?"

"I will be asking for help."

"So, do you know someone that can help you?"

"Happily, yes, yes I do."

"Oh, you will have to get another letter from the hospital authorities to bring someone to help you."

"No, no I don't really think so."

"Look, we might be quite friendly, but I'm sorry, but I can't let you bring in someone without the okay of the hospital."

"That is not being a problem …, the person that I need already has permission to be in the hospital."

"You're sure of that?"

"Of course I am. Totally sure. For you see, the person that I am thinking of, is being you."

"Me? I don't know how to do any of your stuff. I don't know anything about it.

Honestly, I don't even really, totally believe in it. Don't get me wrong, I quite like you as a person, but I'm still not absolutely sure that you're not really some type of a nutta."

"But of course, you are being absolutely right, I am surely what you are calling a nutta."

"Oh, I'm sorry, didn't mean to be so rude."

"No, you are right, I am a nutta, and you know nothing of what I am doing.

But this, I already know, I need your help because you are a person, full of love.

I will show you what to do. If you could be kind enough to help."

"Sure, sure I'll help. So, when do you want to do this?"

"Would now be a good time?"

"Oh, I'll just have to do me rounds again. How long will it take?"

"Not so very long, could fifteen minutes, be possible?"

"Sure, I'll have to ask Sandra, in the next ward to take over my monitors, she's a good 'un, she'll do fifteen minutes, no sweat."

She enters into the chamber; he is sitting cross legged, lost in a circular repetitive chanting of Aum.

Although he seems totally lost in his world, he is still able to notice her entering and to direct her to sit down on a pillow that he had somewhere pilfered.

"Teyata Om Bekanze Bekanze Mahabekanze Bekanze Radza Samutgate Soha."

"Please, I will be teaching you some words."

"Okay."

"Om Mani Padme Hum."

"I don't understand."

"Om Mani Padme Hum, it means 'the jewel is in the heart of the lotus."

It is in a language, Sanskrit, please try to repeat it."

"Om Mani Padme Hum."

"Oh mammy, put me bum." She starts to giggle. "Sorry, just couldn't help it, could say it again, please?"

"Om…(Om)… Mani… (Mani)... Padme…(Padme)… Hum…(Hum)"

"Don't be worrying if you are not very sure of the words, we will be singing them one hundred and six times

"You're joking."

"Please can you place your hands, here."

"On the sternum?"

"Yes, there, near the heart.

Please, thinking of love and opening of the heart."

And then he begins; Om Mani Padme Hum."
"
She joins in, and follows him, as best she can.

They continue for some time before he gets up, still singing, and places a medium sized bowl on the same point on the patient's upper chest.

He bowl is balanced on the back of her hand.

The bowl sounds an 'F', and resonates gently for a short while.

He strikes the bowl again, and again, and again, and again.

Eventually, he looks towards the nurse, who, while still singing, never-the-less, has begun to drift away.

She notices his attention, and as he begins to chant, more and more softly, she follows his lead and quietens her own input.

He removes her hand from under the bowl and directs her to go and sit.

They are in silence.

He gently sounds the bowl, one more time, and goes to sit, this time in total silence.

She is much too scared and in awe to make any sound, or even movement, so she just sits and waits until.

"Namaste," he brings his hands together, in the classic position of pray, and salutes her, bending ever so slightly his head, inclined towards her.

"Namaste," she responds.

She repeats his gesture, then, silently, he nods to her, and indicates the door.

She gets up, impressed, goes to the door, takes one last look at the 'nutta', and goes back to perform, her regular, assigned tasks.

## 17. Dealing with the Wreckage

My head ached terribly the next morning.

I was all stiff and scrunched up.

I hadn't made it to the bedroom, I had just crumpled onto the first soft object that presented itself, that being the hall couch.

No-one had thought or dared to waken me, and so I wondered into the dining room well after everyone had finished breakfast, or so I thought.

Unfortunately my nemesis had decided to continue to squat the piece, still scrutinising the business section, he was likely on his third pot of coffee.

"Ah James, so civil to join me for a fresh cup of coffee," he rang the bell and ordered another fresh pot.

His ability to accept or ignore the last night's altercation was fascinating, but I remembered that it was far from the first time that this had happened.

"What's going to happen to me?"

"In what way me boy?"

"I have no job and no money."

"It's never been that much of a problem in the past."

"I wasn't thirty years old then."

"Thirty, oh my, we're all getting older, aren't we?"

"But what am I to do, where am I to go?" I felt as lost as Alice, and just as confused.

"What-ever you want, where-ever you want," thus speaks the Cheshire Cat.

"But I have no job, nor any money."

"James, we are not poor, you will always have a roof over your head, food in your belly and enough money to get pissed when-ever you feel the need."

I looked closely at him to see if I could ascertain any sarcasm or mockery in his voice or his attitude.

But there was none, he was being totally sincere, even kind and generous.

The old crocodile, who had coldly and maliciously snapped off my leg, just the night before, was inviting me to share his catch with him for breakfast.

"I'm going out for a smoke."

"Take your jacket it's a wee bit chilly out." And I did.

I was back up the oak tree, my second cigarette already burnt out, when she called up to me.

"Bonjour monsieur," she was alone. She startled me.

"Sorry." She became nervous and panicky.

"It's okay, I just didn't hear you coming, its fine."

I turned to face the beautiful young lady with flaming hair and raven eyes.

"What are you doing here?"

"Oh I come here quite a lot, not many other kids come here, I come when I need to be alone."

"Do you want me to leave?"

"You were here first."

This was the first time that we had ever had a conversation.

"If you need to be alone."

"Why are you here, up my tree?"

'This has been my tree since long before you were born."

What gave her the courage to confront me in this way? As if somewhere she was testing me.

But the testing didn't end there.

"You been smoking?" She picked up a fresh stub from under the tree.

"And if I had?"

"Strike me a fag, will ya'?"

"Are you serious?"

"Sure."

"But you're only," I took a moment to calculate, "twelve."

"And a half."

"You're much too young to smoke."

"Jay says that you started smoking at eleven."

I was particularly shocked by both the information and the source of it, not to mention my surprise at the way she referred to him.

"You call him Jay?"

"Sure, why not? Didn't you used to call him Jay?"

"I did."

"But you don't no more?"

"Not any-more." I corrected.

"Not any more, Mr. Ferguson." Her lack of respect was intentional.

"Do you see much of Jay, of Jean Jacques?"

"From time to time, especially Christmas and Easter, of course."

"Why, of course?"

" 'Cus he brings us presents."

"And why do you think that he brings you presents?"

I was quite interested to hear the response to this one.

"To begin with, he would say that Father Christmas or the Easter Bunny kept bringing them to the works.

By mistake, he said, 'cus Angie and me were there most of the time.

We had decorated the tree or made stuff for the bunny there.

But then I sussed that it was the parents that bought the pres'es, so he had to come up with another story.

Then he said that it was a special thing from the works, 'cus mum was a single parent, and it was the same for all single parents.'

"So do you believe that?"

"Course not, it's a crock 'o shit."

"So why do you think that he brings these things?"

"I first thought it was just that he fancied her, but then he got engaged to 'Ellen, so that didn't seem to make sense.

And I watch how they are together, they're nice and friendly together, but they don't touch, not even by accident.

Y' know, when people fancy each other, they often touch, even when they shouldn't, so they do it by accident, they don't."

"So, what's your thinking now?"

"You know what's queer?"

"No what's queer?"

"Two straight men in a gay bar."

"What?"

"Sor' it's just a daft joke, couldn't help miself. What's queer is that if you look closely, I got the same eyes and nose as Jay."

"And?"

"I was thinking, that maybe, one night, that they both got totally rat-arsed, and screwed like crazy, and then nine months later, this little miracle arrived."

"So you believe that Jay is your real father?"

"For all of five minutes."

"And now?"

"I've seen how you look at Angie, every time you meet.

I've felt how she squeezes me 'and, when you're there. Jay never fucked her, but I'd bet me life, it was you that did."

"And?"

"Well, then, that makes you me dad."

"How long have thought this?"

"Long enough."

"But have you told anybody?"

"Whose t' tell?"

"And now?"

"And now, strike me a fag, and you can also spot me a twenty, dad."

And so our relationship began.

Little was I to know that that cigarette and twenty pound note would be the first steps towards alcoholism, drug dependency and prostitution.

All due to my stupid need to compensate for not being the father that I wished to be.

The daughter that I loved more than all the world was about to destroy her whole life, and I was the unconscious orchestrator and supporter of this.

If the path to Hell is paved with good intentions, then emotional compensations build themselves a five lane highway.

Gentle reader, thank you for purchasing this book and I very much hope that you have enjoyed it.

If so, please help others to make the choice to read this by sharing your views with your friends and writing a review on Amazon.


Thank you,

Kindest regards

Gary

# Other works

## By

## Gary Edward Gedall

# Island of Serenity Book 1
# The Island of Survival

Pierre-Alain James 'Faron' Ferguson is about to commit suicide, in his suicide note he attempts to understand how he has come to have wrecked not only his own life, but also all of those around him.

Pierre-Alain James 'Faron' Ferguson finds himself in a type of 'no-mans-land', between here and there, he must accept to visit the 7 islands before he will be allowed to continue on to his next steps. The islands are named; Survival, Pleasure, Esteem, Love, Expression, Insight and lastly, the Island of Serenity

**The Early Years:**
Pierre-Alain James 'Faron' Ferguson is born into a well-to-do household of a factory owner, Scottish father and mother of a noble French family

He, and his younger brother Jay, grow up in a home of two distant but invested parents. Already, the first, small stones of his future problems are being put into place.

**The Island of Survival:**
Faron finds himself on the first of the seven islands, transformed into a prehistoric human form, he must learn how to interact with the local environment and the early humanoid tribe.

Here, he must reconnect with his instinct of survival.

# Island of Serenity Book 2
## Sun & Rain

This is the second chapter of Faron's life history, in which he falls in love, becomes a real cowboy, starts boarding school, finds his two best friends, and more than that would be telling too much.

FREE: If you have not yet read Book 1, Survival, no worries, I have included a shortened version, so as to introduce you to the story and the main characters.

## Island of Serenity Book 3
# The Island of Pleasure
## Vol 1
## Venice

### Part 1.

Faron finds himself in a past version of Venice, as the
owner of an old but grand hotel that doubles as the
meeting place for the wealthy men of the City and the high
class escort girls that live in the establishment.

Faron can do anything that he likes without limitation or
cost. Not only can he avail himself of the girls, but can eat
and drink, without limit, but never suffer from a hangover,
nor gain a gram.

So why has the enigmatic guide brought him here, and
will his limitless access to life's offerings really bring him
the pleasure that he is destined to experience?

### Part 2.

 Faron is transformed into an adolescent tom boy. In this
more modern version of Venice, 'he' has just 7 days to be
made into a high class escort girl.

What does this experience and the intrigues of the other
persons within his sphere, mean for him, on his continuing
quest to understand, and to experience, Pleasure?

## Island of Serenity Book 4
# The Island of Pleasure
## (Vol 2)
## Japan

Faron finds himself in the mystery of a long ago Japan, in the body of a young, trainee Geisha.

Who is this sad, young man that he must help to find back his pleasure in life?

Why must he hide the identity of his mother, from the rest of the world?

Why was the love of his mother's life, stolen away by her sister, known to all as Madame Butterfly?

What part does the feudal lord of the region have in all this?

And how does Faron finally succeed to find the key to rediscovering pleasure in his life?

# *Tasty Bites*

(Series – published or in preproduction)

*Face to Face*

A young teacher asks to befriend an older colleague on Face Book, "I have a very delicate situation, for which I would appreciate your advice"

*Free 2 Luv*

The e-mail exchanges between; RichBitch, SecretLover, the mother, the bestie, and the lawyer, expose a complicated and surprising story

*Heresy*

An e-mail from a future controlled by the major pharmaceutical companies, "please do what you can to change this situation, now, before it happens …

*Love you to death*    A toy town parable,
populated by your favourite
playthings, about the
dangerous game of
dependency and co-
dependency

*Master of all Masters*    In an ancient land,
the disciples argue about
who is the Master of all
Masters. The solution is to
create a competition

**Pandora's Box**    If you had a magic box,
into which you could
bury all your negative
thoughts and feelings,
wouldn't that be
wonderful?

*Shame of a family*    Being born different can
be a heavy burden to
bear.
Especially for the family

*The Noble Princess*    If you were just a humble
Saxon, would you be
good enough to marry a
noble Norman Princess?

*The Ugly Barren Fruit Tree*   A weird foreign tree that bears no fruit, in an apple orchard. What value can it possibly have?


*The Woman of my Dreams*   What would you do, if the woman that you fell in love with in your dream, suddenly appears in real life?

# Adventures with the Master

Dhargey was a sickly child or so his parents treated him. He was too weak to join the army or work in the fields or even join the monastery as a normal trainee monk.

To explain to the 'Young Master' why he should be accepted into the order with a lightened program, he was forced to accompany the revered old man a little ways up the mountain.

As his parents watched him leave; somewhere they felt that they would never see their sickly, fragile boy ever again, somewhere they were totally right.

**He** was a happy, healthy seven year old until he witnessed the riders, dressed in red and black, destroying his village and murdering his parents; the trauma cut deep into his psyche.

Only the chance meeting with a wandering monk could set him back onto the road towards health and serenity.

Through meditation, initiations, stories, taming wild horses, becoming a monkey, mastering the staff and the sword; the future 'Young Master' prepares to face his greatest demon.

Two men, two journeys, one goal.

# The Tales of
# Peter the Pixie

Peter the innocent, honest, young pixie, and his friends; Elli, the, 'much older then she looks', modest but powerful Fairy, Timothy, the old, trustworthy, Toad and the, ever so noble, Fire Dragon, are the best of friends.

Together, they experience many wonderful and heart-warming adventures.

Told in a classical children's story style; Peter and his friends, meet all kinds of creatures and situations.

As with all children, Peter is often confronted with experiences that he does not know how best to deal with, and he often reacts in ways that are not the most appropriate. Fortunately; with the help of his good friends, good will and common sense, everything always turns out for the best.

# None Fiction:

## The Zen Approach to Modern Living Vol 1

### Fundamentals, Family & Friends

Life is often experienced as a series of conflicts and aggressions, both from the outside and within ourselves.

The Zen Approach to Modern Living series, will lead you towards a more harmonious way of dealing with the many, complex and competing elements of your daily life.

These conflicts leave us exhausted, depressed, angry, and feeling generally unhappy and unfulfilled.

Being more in harmony with yourself will bring more happiness, more energy and open up the route to self-fulfillment.

Volume 1 covers; an introduction to the basic concepts, our relationship with ourselves, our family, (partner, children, parents, brothers, sisters and in-laws), friends and enemies.

Plus, plus, plus, A Bonus Chapter: My Deepest, Darkest, Secret.

# The Zen approach to Low Impact Training and Sports

## A simple method for achieving a healthy body and a healthy mind

Many of us approach our fitness and sports activities in an aggressive and competitive fashion.

And even if we feel that we succeed to break out of our comfort zones and win against ourselves or our opponent, there is an important cost to bear.

This level of violence that we have come to accept, so as to reach our goals is also an aggression against ourselves. By removing this need to 'win at any price', and tuning in with our bodies and emotions, we can achieve an enormous amount, all the while being in harmony with our mind, body and spirit.

The Zen approach to Low Impact Training and Sports, is a new softer approach where you can have the best of all worlds.

# REMEMBER

Stories and poems for self-help and self-development
based on techniques of Ericksonian and auto-hypnosis

*Dusk falls, the world shrinks little by little into a smaller and
smaller circle as the light continues to diminish.*

*The centre of this world is illuminated by a small, crackling
sun; the flames dance, and the rough faces of the people
gathered there are lit by the fire of their expectations.*

*The old man will begin to speak, he will explain to them how
the world is, how it was, how it was created. He will help them
understand how things have a sense, an order, a way that they
need to be.*

*He will clarify the sources of un-wellness and unhappiness,
what is sickness, where it comes from, how to notice it and...
how to heal it.*

*To heal the sick, he will call forth the forces of the invisible
realms, maybe he will sing, certainly he will talk, and talk, and
talk.*

Since the beginning of time we have gathered round those
who can bring us the answers to our questions and the means
to alleviate our sufferings.

This practice has not fundamentally changed since the earliest
times; in every era, continent and culture we have found and
continue to find these experiences.

In this, amongst the oldest of the healing traditions, he has
succeeded to meld modern therapy theories and techniques with
stories and poems of the highest quality.

With much humanity, clinical vignettes, common sense and lots
of humour, the reader is gently carried from situation to
situation. Whether the problems described concern you directly,
indirectly or not at all, you will surely find interest and benefits
from the wealth of insights and advices contained within and the
conscious or unconscious positive changes through reading the
stories and poems.

# Picturing the Mind

## Vol 1

**A simple model capable to explain the functioning and dysfunctioning of the human psyche.**

## Introduction to the Field theory of Human Functioning

For the average man and woman in the street, the complex and competing theories and models of the human psyche; its development, functioning and dis-functioning are often unhelpful for their understanding of themselves.

This becomes even more problematic when they find themselves in difficulty, as often, even the mental health professionals, who are experts in their own fields, find themselves at a loss to communicate successfully how and why the patent is unwell and what needs to happen to find or regain a healthy balance.

This opens up the question; 'is it possible to image a simple, single model, accessible to everyone, to explain the development, functioning and dis-functioning of the human psyche?'

One that builds on existing theories and models, benefitting from the mass of experience and research of 'modern western' psychological concepts and ideas, but also integrating traditional visions of the human psyche and modern theories from the physical sciences.

Picturing the Mind, is an attempt to answer to this need.

# Picturing the Mind
## Vol 2

The second volume following on from the initial concepts will reflect on such subjects as:

Relationships
Exchanging energy
Heart & Soul
Recuperation
Subjective constructions
An unconscious yes, an unconscious no
Me, myself and everyone else
Circles in circles, the micro level
Circles in circles, the macro level
Intuition
Metaphysical reflections

# Picturing the Mind

## Vol 3

Will deal with:

Psychopathology

Traditional psychotherapy
&
Alternative therapeutic approaches.